Couple's Night

By: Jessica Terry

COUPLE'S NIGHT

First edition. September 6, 2025.

Copyright © 2025 Jessica Terry.

ISBN: 979-8999506924

Written by Jessica Terry.

To my family, friends, readers, fellow authors, and anyone else who has shown love and support, I appreciate you.

Content warning: cheating, divorce, and mention of miscarriage (off-page).

Chapter 1

Serenity Cook & Taj Wharton

If only there was some guarantee that she wouldn't have to worry about avoiding sex when she got home....

It had been a day. As much as Serenity Cook enjoyed owning her own café, this was one of those days that made part of her wish she just had a regular job and didn't have to be in charge. Being the boss was draining.

She and her employees were wrapping things up for the day when she got a call from her boyfriend, Taj. It brought the first smile she'd had in hours.

"Hey, sweetie," she greeted him, easing back into the kitchen prep area for some privacy. "You have no idea how glad I am to hear your voice right now."

"Rough day, huh?"

"It just seemed to go on forever. Every time I looked at the clock, it's like it barely moved."

"I know how that is. You're gonna be able to leave soon, though, right?"

"Thankfully. Rosie and Vern are out there getting everything closed out and cleaned up."

"Nice. Well, I'll probably beat you getting home, so what do you want for dinner? Or did you eat already?"

"I haven't." Serenity grabbed a sponge and cleaned the edge of the stainless steel sink. "Do you feel like making your famous cheesesteaks? I'd *love* one of those."

"Maybe," Taj teased. "Do I get to help you work off those calories later?"

Her smile fading, Serenity's hand dropped the sponge. "You know what? On second thought, that might, um, that might be a little too heavy for me tonight. How about we just keep it light with a salad or something?"

There was a pause, and she hoped Taj didn't call her out on her deflection. She knew he recognized the change in her tone, because it happened just about every time he tried to entice her with sexual innuendo. And she just didn't have the energy for this particular conversation tonight.

"Fine," he finally replied, his tone flat. "I think we have some shrimp or something I can sauté to go on top of it."

"That sounds great."

"Before I forget, I saw Rasheed earlier. He mentioned he hadn't talked to you in a minute."

"Oh..." A cold wave washed over Serenity, and she was glad this conversation was happening over the phone. She didn't have the greatest poker face and she knew Taj would pick up on her discomfort at the mention of Rasheed's name. Serenity had been avoiding Rasheed for weeks and knew she wasn't ready to tell Taj why that was.

"I'm sure I'll see him soon enough," she managed to respond evenly. Sad part was, she knew she would. Rasheed was part of her close circle of friends, and she wouldn't be able to avoid him forever. She could only hope to keep it together when they were in the same room. "We've all got a lot going on."

"I guess. Well, I'm almost at the house; I'm gonna take a shower and then get the dinner together. It should be ready by the time you get here. Send me a text when you're leaving."

"I will. See you soon. Love you."

"Love you, too."

Serenity expelled a deep breath as she ended the call. She didn't know how much longer she'd be able to keep this up. She'd been with Taj for three years; he deserved better.

Putting it out of her mind for the moment, she resumed her end-of-the-night tasks. She hated that she was actually nervous to go home. All she could do was pray that Taj didn't bring up Rasheed again.

When she got home a while later, Taj was putting the finishing touches on dinner. Serenity took a quick shower before joining him in the kitchen of the townhouse they shared, forcing a relaxed countenance. She didn't want Taj grilling her about what was on her mind.

He pulled her to him as soon as she entered the room and laid a deep kiss on her, holding her close. Her arms slid around his neck, her fingers snaking through his short locs. Her body warmed as his tongue stroked hers, and when his hands slid underneath her oversized shirt that reached her mid-thighs, she resisted the urge to stop him. It wasn't that it didn't feel good; she loved how Taj touched her. It was the next part that she was dreading.

But when he kissed down her neck to her shoulder, his thumbs hooking into the top of her bikini-cut panties and sliding them down, her reservations faded. She whimpered against his lips, grabbing fistfuls of his shirt.

"I've been looking forward to seeing you all day," he muttered, squeezing her fleshy bottom. He pressed a lingering kiss to her lips as he lightly pinched her hardened nipple through her shirt, causing her to gasp. "I hope you don't mind if we put off dinner for a minute."

Only able to shake her head, Serenity's jaw fell open as Taj slid a hand between her legs, circling his roughened fingers around her clit. Her legs widened without him having to ask, releasing a loud groan when he slipped a couple of fingers inside of her.

Taj loved how she was responding to him. He braced himself for her suddenly pumping the brakes; sometimes she let him have his way with her while other times she'd stop him abruptly, even though she was enjoying it. When he'd ask her about it, she'd just awkwardly change the subject. He usually let it go, but his curiosity about the reasoning behind her sporadic skittishness was about to boil over like soup in an overheated pot. She didn't act like that for no reason.

But the way she was moving her hips against his hand, he figured maybe this would be one of the nights she indulged him. The realization emboldening him, he quickly and smoothly slipped her shirt over her head, leaving all of her luscious brown body on display. He loved Serenity's cocoa brown skin; it was one of the first things he'd noticed about her when they met. It seemed to glow, no matter where she was or what she was doing.

"Get on the counter," he ordered breathlessly, already backing her towards it with his lithe body.

She hesitated, glancing back at it. Taj felt an automatic pinch between his eyebrows, anticipating her shutting him down.

"How about the chair instead?" she suggested, pointing.

Relieved, Taj wordlessly guided her to the nearest kitchen chair, pausing as she quickly covered it with her shirt onto it before sitting. Taj immediately dropped to his knees, pushing one of her legs wider and lifting the other over his shoulder. Not in the mood for teasing, he dove his face between her legs, wasting no time sliding his tongue along her deliciously wet folds and earning a hard shudder. He pulled her hips closer to the chair edge so he could get his tongue where he wanted it, which was inside of her. He loved being inside of her, any way he could get there.

"Ooh, Taj..." Serenity's hands gripped his hair as she slowly wound against his mouth. The hair on his chin brushed her inner thigh, sending another ripple through her. Anything that had been on her mind was forgotten; she loved how he touched her, savored her. Taj was only the second lover she'd ever had, but of the two, he was definitely the best. "Yes, Taj..."

His hand slid up to grab her aching breast, loving that she had way more than his hand could hold. Serenity's ample breasts had assisted in many a nighttime fantasy for him, even after they got together. When she got stingy with his access, he could at least imagine them.

He continued to slowly suck on her clit, his own arousal building the closer she got to orgasm. Her body began to shake and he knew she was getting close.

"Oh my god," she whimpered, her hips moving faster. "That feels amazing; please don't stop..."

Taj just moaned as he continued to pleasure her, savoring her with his tongue while his fingers teased and tweaked her nipple. He winced as her grip on his hair tightened, and her moans ascended into squeaky territory, signaling her oncoming orgasm. He slowly slid the flat of his tongue from the bottom to the top before teasing her clit until she exploded.

"*Taj!*" she screamed, her body jerking and convulsing. Her back arched as her head fell over the back of the chair, the grip on Taj's hair loosening. Her body felt like it was melting as she caught her breath.

Still horny, Taj leaned up to kiss her soft, heaving stomach before taking her nipple into his mouth. She immediately sat up and pushed him away.

"I'm too sensitive," Serenity admonished, still breathless. She stopped his hand that had been kneading her hip. "I need a minute."

Taj sucked his lips in as the instant frustration overtook his arousal. He knew what 'I need a minute' meant; Serenity was likely done with anything amorous for the rest of the night. After she came, she didn't want to be touched. And usually, she wasn't in the mood to do any touching on him, either.

But he tried to keep hope alive as he wordlessly stood, eyes on her. She was so beautiful to him, her short natural hair, sparkling brown eyes and bright white teeth displayed by her beautiful smile drawing him in from the moment he saw her four years ago. He especially loved watching her when she was coming down off an intense orgasm. When she allowed herself to be, she was extremely responsive and expressive, and he loved her like that. It was when she held back that irritated him. At this point in their relationship, there should've been no holding back on anything, in his opinion.

Finally, she opened her eyes and looked up at him. He was still eying her hungrily, biting his bottom lip, silently willing her to pull his basketball shorts down and return the favor. It had been way too long since he felt Serenity's lips on his dick and he was surely aching for it now, but knew what would happen if he just came out and asked for it. She had to initiate it on her own.

Serenity knew what he wanted. It was what he always wanted after he went down on her. Her eyes dropped to his crotch, seeing the obvious evidence of his arousal through his shorts. She swallowed as nervousness overtook her and she quickly stood, grabbing her shirt.

"I'm ready to eat; how 'bout you?" she asked, avoiding his eyes as she slipped the nightshirt back over her head and stuck her yellow fingernails into her hair, mindlessly massaging her scalp. "My stomach is growling. Are those artichokes? I *love* artichokes."

Taj resisted the urge to curse as he turned away from her. He ran a hand down his face, silently telling himself not to trip. It was a speech he was all too used to giving himself, especially in the last year or so.

"Yeah," he finally grunted. He went to the sink to wash his hands, not trusting himself to say anything else.

Serenity could tell he was frustrated, and she hated herself for it. Taj was so good to her and she knew he wasn't satisfied with how things were between them, namely their sex life. But he was thankfully patient with her, which she needed. At some point they had settled into an unspoken agreement that this was just how things were.

They sat down to a spinach, shrimp, and artichoke salad, with Serenity indulging in a glass of white wine while Taj just opted for grapefruit juice. Their stilted conversation stuck to safe subjects like work and things in the news, only perking up when they began talking about their friends. It was way easier to talk about other people's issues.

"Lavinia said the renovations on her and Ricky's house are finally done," Serenity commented, taking a sip of her wine. "She praised their contractor and the job he did, especially with all of her specifications. Now it's on to redecorating."

"I bet Ricky had little to no say in whatever was done," Taj muttered. "She never listens to what he wants."

"I wouldn't go that far."

"Everybody knows that. She bulldozes him and he just goes along with it to keep the peace. After growing up with parents that were always at each other's throats, it's almost automatic for him to just fall back instead of arguing about stuff."

"Lavinia *is* rather strong-willed. But I know she loves Ricky more than anything."

"If you say so. But everybody has a breaking point; it's only a matter of time before she pushes him to his."

Serenity wondered where Taj's breaking point was, and how close he was to reaching it. She wasn't delusional enough to think that he was totally happy in their relationship. But it had become easier for them to pretend that everything was fine than broach the hard conversation.

"Hopefully he realizes how much she loves him, even if she has some flaws," she said softly, her fork toying with a piece of shrimp on her plate. She prayed that Taj realized she was talking about the two of them as much as she was talking about their friends.

Taj looked up at her as he chewed, but didn't comment. They continued to eat in silence for several moments before he spoke again.

"I was thinking of having everyone over soon," he announced. He took a long swig of his juice. "We haven't all hung out in a little while."

"Oh..." Serenity tried to tamp down her instant anxiety. "What is it you wanna do?"

"I don't know, but something different than just us all having dinner or watching movies. We need to switch things up."

"Sounds good," she made herself say. "Rasheed and Iman, too?"

He frowned slightly. "Of course. Why not?"

Serenity fought like hell to keep her face even. "Iman is my girl. But her and Rasheed together usually just leads to a bunch of drama, especially once you factor in alcohol."

"Those two aren't half as bad as Charmaine and Ace. And Lavinia is enough drama all by herself. We can't leave 'Sheed and Iman out; they're our people."

"Right. Of course."

Taj got up to put his plate in the sink while Serenity chugged her wine, draining the glass. The thought of an evening with Rasheed almost made her itch. She loved all of her friends dearly, but being around Rasheed made her uncomfortable. And while she knew she would eventually have to fess up as to why, she was in no hurry to do so.

Chapter 2

Charmaine Mills & Ace Middleton

Charmaine knew her face was still red from anger. She couldn't believe Ace had said what he did.

"Babe, have you ever considered getting a boob job?" he'd asked earlier, drinking orange juice right out of the jug. He licked his lips as his narrowed eyes studied her small chest. "You don't have to settle for those things like they are, you know."

Charmaine's jaw dropped at his gall. "Excuse me?"

He shrugged. "I'm just saying; wouldn't you want to have bigger titties? Like Serenity's; that girl has some *amazing* breasts. Even though you're way skinnier than her, I bet those would still look good on you."

"Ace!"

"What? Okay, maybe not quite as big as hers; she's probably a good triple-D. Hell, she might be an E...how does all that go, again?"

He seemed oblivious to her rapidly-growing ire as he plunked the top back onto the orange juice and returned it to the refrigerator. Then he strolled over, grabbed her waist as he gave her a quick fruity kiss, and headed to the living room, actually whistling.

Charmaine had stood there fuming for so long that she heard the basketball game Ace was loudly enjoying go into halftime. She finally stalked to their bedroom, cutting her eyes at him as she passed, not that he noticed. He was too busy going into his usual spiel about how he'd be smoking everybody on the court if he hadn't hurt his knee in high school.

Now, Charmaine stood leaning over the bathroom sink in their en suite, trying to calm herself down. It wasn't like Ace's insensitivity was anything new. The man had almost no filter, at least when it came to her. And ever since they got engaged, his lips had gotten even more loose, as if he felt that her accepting his marriage proposal entitled him to say whatever he wanted.

She was sitting on their bed absently flipping through one of her E. Lynn Harris novels when Ace entered the room. He plopped down beside her, causing her to bounce and almost drop her book.

"Babe, did I tell you about the latest idea I had for my restaurant?" he asked excitedly.

Subtly rolling her eyes, she droned, "No, but I'm sure you'll-"

"I think I'm gonna have my main thing be savory waffles," he forged ahead. "Everybody does the regular kind. And I'm trying to rival Toast and Butter."

Charmaine shook her head. Toast and Butter was a pancake house in town and they stayed bustling, thanks to their thick fluffy pancakes and syrups that were made fresh every day. She didn't want to say how tall an order it was for Ace to think he was going to rival them, especially any time soon.

And especially since Ace wasn't even a chef. He worked in architecture, but had gotten it in his head that opening a restaurant was a good idea. And after watching so many people become famous on social media by cooking in their own kitchens, Ace was convinced there was no reason he couldn't do the same. But he wasn't satisfied with just doing live videos while he experimented with his waffle recipes; he had to go big and open a whole waffle restaurant.

Charmaine thought it was a ridiculous idea. Ace didn't know the first thing about running a restaurant, no matter how many articles he'd read about it. He insisted that he could just hire people who knew what they were doing and he'd just be the overseer. It freaked Charmaine out that he was so willing to sink a load of money into something that would likely fail in mere months when they were planning a life together. His carelessness was both appalling and frightening.

Instead of voicing her concerns, though, she just sighed and closed her book. "You do remember our cake tasting appointment tomorrow, right?"

"Yeah." He affectionately rubbed her thigh, smiling at her. "What time is it, again?"

"Three o'clock."

"Cool. I'll meet you there 'cause I have a meeting at one."

"You think you'll be late?"

"I shouldn't be."

"And Taj wants us to come over this weekend," she informed him. "I think he said something about a game night. He's invited the whole crew."

"Dope. That should be fun; we haven't all hung out in a while. Somebody usually has some excuse why they can't make it."

"Yeah. But he assured me Serenity and Lavinia will be there; they're usually the ones with the conflicts."

"Hmm." Ace removed the book from her hand and tossed it to the floor before yanking her down by the legs and climbing on top of her with a mischievous smirk. He licked his thick lips. "How 'bout I get you up outta these jeans?"

Despite herself, a smile tugged at Charmaine's lips. She both loved and hated how she could never seem to resist Ace's charms. She knew she needed to speak on her concerns about his restaurant aspirations (and call him out on his boob job suggestion from earlier) but when he put his hands or lips on her, all rational thought tended to pause. And with the way he pulled down the straps of her tank top and bra and started placing loud kisses to her breasts before sucking her nipples with a satisfied moan, she figured he couldn't have been *too* unhappy with her B-cup breasts as they were.

Before too long, she was writhing underneath him as they kissed wildly, her shirt and bra pushed down to her waist and Ace's shirt tossed to the floor. Her concerns were temporarily forgotten; all she cared about was getting Ace inside of her.

And when they were both finally naked and Ace slid his beautiful long brown length into her, Charmaine had no worries. She just wrapped her thin legs around his waist and held on tight for what she knew as coming.

"Damn, I can't wait to make you my wife," Ace grunted, pounding into her. He always went full throttle, going from zero to sixty with no slow and easy in between. That was how it had always been with him. He gave a hard smack to her hip. "I love you so much, Charmaine."

"I love you, too," she managed to respond, her locked ankles falling apart.

"Fuck," he muttered, burying his face in her neck. She yelped when his teeth sank into her soft skin. "I can't wait 'til you have my son. *Fuck*, you feel so good!"

Charmaine responded by pushing him onto his back and mounting him, instantly resuming their usual frenetic pace. She braced her hands on his strong chest and just concentrated on ushering them both to climax. Charmaine had never been one for being very vocal during sex, but Ace talked enough for the both of them.

When they had each been thoroughly pleased, she collapsed next to him on the rumpled sheets. She was about to lay her head on his chest when he pulled her to him and planted a sloppy kiss on her lips before rolling off the bed.

"I'm gonna go meet up with Ricky," he informed, swiping a hand down his sweaty face. "He's been going through it with Lavinia, so I offered to take him out for some drinks."

Biting back her disappointment, Charmaine just ran a hand through her thin brown hair, feeling her slightly damp roots. It reminded her that she needed a touch-up. "And you have to leave *now*?"

"I don't wanna be late, babe," he retorted, glancing at his watch. "And I don't put it past Ricky to dip out if he beats us there."

"Us? Are Rasheed and Taj going, too?"

"Rasheed probably will; not sure about Taj." Ace headed into the bathroom. "You don't have to worry about fixing anything for me for dinner; we'll just eat while we're out."

Charmaine sighed, pulling the sheet around her damp body. "Fine. Whatever."

The shower came on a moment later, with Ace alternating between whistling and blasting the lyrics to some rap song. Charmaine thought about joining him in the shower but decided against it, opting to leave well enough alone. There was no telling what time he'd get home later and she figured they might as well end their time together on a good note.

A half hour later, Ace was freshly showered and dressed in a throwback Chicago Bulls jersey and jeans. He hurried over to the bed where she was still lounging and gave her a peck.

"Love you," he said, winking at her. "Don't wait up."

I wasn't going to, anyway, she thought to herself as he strode out the door. She just turned to her side as she heard the front door close, wondering for the hundredth time if this was the kind of life she really wanted to sign up for.

"I'm *so* sorry," Charmaine expressed again, glancing at her watch. She was at the popular bakery Pure Sugar for her and Ace's cake tasting, except Ace wasn't there. Charmaine called him three times, repeatedly getting sent to voicemail. Her face burned with embarrassment.

"His meeting must have run long," she continued in explanation, casting an apologetic glance to Peaches, the bakery's owner. "I guess he doesn't have his phone on..."

"Don't worry about it, baby," Peaches replied soothingly. "Things come up."

Charmaine hoped it was as simple as that and not a case of Ace just flaking on her. He had a tendency to change his mind about things at times and not let her know. But she thought they'd gotten past that particular issue months ago. "Still, you prepared all of this for us, and you all stay so busy...I know you don't have time to waste."

"You're here; it's not wasted. We can continue without him or you can take these samples home and just let me know what the two of you decide on. Either way, Tango can handle things while I'm over here with you."

Blushing immediately at the mention of Peaches' son that was loading cupcakes into a box at the front counter, Charmaine took a sip of her water. She'd been harboring a crush on Tango since the first time she walked into Pure Sugar and saw him manning the counter, and she couldn't deny that her love of sweets wasn't the only thing that had her in that bakery at least once a week. There was something about that hulk of a man, whose bulging muscles were littered with various tattoos and who always wore a Yankees baseball cap turned backwards, dishing out sugary pastries day in and day out. And every time he flashed that single-dimpled smile at her, it sent a jolt right to her middle.

And he might've made an appearance in a late-night fantasy or two.

"I appreciate it, Peaches," she finally replied. "I'll take these home and get Ace's opinion then call you tomorrow with what we decide."

"That'll be just fine. I'll get these samples packed up for you."

"Thanks so much."

Peaches stood and grabbed the tray holding the beautifully prepared wedding cake samples and headed to the back. Charmaine contemplated calling Ace again as she drained her cup of water.

"You want some more?"

She jumped, glancing up to see Tango standing over her, gracing her with that enticing smile of his.

"Umm, huh?"

"Your water." He motioned towards her empty cup. "Can I get you some more?"

"Oh...I'm okay, thanks."

"No problem." He pulled the towel that was draped over his shoulder and wiped away the few cake crumbs that littered the small round table. Standing, he gave her a wink. "You know where to find me if you need anything."

"Yeah..." She bit her lip as he walked away, resisting the urge to admire his impressive backside. There was something about him wearing that apron...

Catching herself, she shook her head to clear it. She didn't need to be lusting after Tango or any other man that wasn't Ace. Even if he *had* stood her up without so much as a phone call.

Armed with her cake samples in Pure Sugar's signature butter yellow box, Charmaine headed out to her car. She tried to call Ace again, but still got no answer.

"I cannot believe him!" she muttered once she got into her car. It briefly crossed her mind that something might be wrong, but she'd experienced this enough with Ace to know that it was likely just a case of him being inconsiderate. She could only guess what excuse it would be this time; his meeting ran long...his phone was on silent...he'd double-booked...or the classic, he forgot.

Needing reassurance, she called her friend Iman. She knew Serenity was probably busy at work and Lavinia would somehow make the conversation about her.

"What's up, girl?" Iman greeted a moment later. "How was the cake tasting?"

"A bust."

"What?"

"Ace never showed up," Charmaine verified. "I sat there for almost an hour waiting on him."

"Why would he do that? Is he working or something?"

"He had a meeting earlier but he said he would've been done with that in plenty of time. And of course, he didn't answer the phone any of the times I called."

"And you need tips on what to say when you cuss him out for this, right? 'Cause I'll gladly oblige."

"Not exactly..."

"I hope you *are* planning on telling him off for this instead of just letting it go like you always do."

"You make it sound like I'm a pushover."

"Well..."

Charmaine's jaw dropped. "You really think that about me??"

"Sometimes I wonder who's more of one, you or Ricky. Y'all are pretty much neck-and-neck."

"Oh my god, I am *not* as bad as Ricky. I speak up when I need to."

"Not nearly enough."

"I learned a long time ago I have to pick my battles with Ace. He'll make things into a *huge* issue, going on and on about it until I wanna pull my hair out. Sometimes it's just not worth it to get into it with him."

"And all the while, you're letting him think he can say or do whatever, 'cause you won't call him on it, anyway. Is that really the kind of precedent you want to set for your marriage?"

Charmaine considered her friend's words, knowing they had merit. The truth was, she *had* let Ace get away with too much over the course of their relationship. He could go back and forth with her all day, willing to dig his heels in until he wore her down. Or justify whatever point he was trying to make to high heaven. Charmaine usually ran out of energy for whatever the issue was after a while.

"Iman, I know it doesn't make any sense from the outside looking in. And anyway, it's easy for *you* to pop off and let the chips fall where they may because you don't care if your man stays or goes."

"That's not true."

"Please. You and Rasheed have been fooling around for how long? But both of you insist that you're not in a *relationship*-relationship; it's just a 'casual thing'. Isn't that what you always say?"

"That doesn't mean I don't care about him," Iman argued. "I have feelings for Rasheed."

"But not enough to be his actual girlfriend?"

"If I'm gonna be anything, I'd be his woman. I ain't in high school."

"Whatever."

"This isn't about me, anyway. When Rasheed tells me he's gonna be somewhere or do something, he has enough respect for me to actually do it. You should be able to say the same thing about your man, especially since he's your fiancé."

Conflicted, Charmaine remained quiet. She just eyed the cars pulling in and out of the parking lot.

"Charmaine," Iman called out.

"Yeah."

"I wish you would think about what I'm telling you. Ace is my boy and this isn't about me dogging him. But you haven't looked happy in months. And whether you admit it or not, I know that's at least partially because of Ace. You need to work out the issues you have with him before y'all walk down the aisle, because I hope you don't think things are gonna magically get better once you're married. It doesn't go like that."

Sighing, Charmaine sunk down a little in her seat. "Yeah. You're right."

"You deserve better, girl. But you have to want better for yourself."

Those words stayed on Charmaine's mind for the rest of the afternoon, especially after she scarfed down all of the cake samples before Ace got home later that night.

Chapter 3

Iman Nichols & Rasheed Murphy

"Stop that," Iman giggled, easing away from Rasheed as he nibbled behind her ear. "You know that tickles."

"Does it?" Rasheed grinned as he pulled her back to him, gently pulling her ear between his lips. "I forgot all about that."

"Uh-huh."

She turned in his arms, and they shared a languid kiss. Their naked bodies were buried under Rasheed's shiny black comforter, having just finished an intense round of lovemaking. As soon as Iman had come through the door, they were all over each other. She loved how explosive their connection was. Since the first time they hooked up almost a year earlier, they were so familiar with each other. There was no weirdness after having gone from being just friends to friends with benefits. Everything about it felt natural, to both of them.

"You sure know how to make a brotha's morning," Rasheed commented, lazily trailing his lips up and down the side of her neck after she'd turned and nestled her back to his front again. "I'm not even mad about having to go in to work today."

"Glad I can be a bright spot."

He knew she was teasing, but Rasheed was tempted to tell her that she really *was* a bright spot for him. They hooked up a few times a week, the frequency having steadily increased in the previous months. Rasheed always looked forward to their time together, even though he felt he had to act like he didn't.

"You have plans later?" he finally asked. "Then I can end my day on a good note, too."

"Aww damn, I wish I could. I told Charmaine I'd hang out with her tonight. She's kinda bummed about some stuff with Ace and I wanted to try to cheer her up."

"Oh." Rasheed tried to hide his disappointment. "That's cool."

They laid there in silence, with Rasheed nuzzling her neck and Iman stroking his arm that was clamped around her middle. Iman really did hate that she already had plans; truth be told, she would've rather spent the evening in Rasheed's bed. She'd begun craving him at some point, and she didn't hate it. But she didn't want to freak him out by admitting that.

"I can cancel," she finally offered, her voice soft.

Rasheed smiled, glad that Iman couldn't see his face. "Yeah?"

"Yeah. I mean, if you want. Charmaine will understand."

Even though he wanted to say the opposite, he heard himself say, "You don't have to do that. Hang with your girl; knowing how Ace is, I can just imagine she's probably going through it."

"Yeah." Iman was slightly deflated, but fixed her expression before turning in his arms, smiling as she pulled his face to hers for a kiss. He immediately pulled her closer, their lips and tongues mingling languidly, neither in any hurry for it to end. His hand caressed her face before snaking into her long black and grey braids, moaning against her lips.

"Well, since I can't see you later on, how 'bout we go another round for the road?" He rolled on top of her. "Might as well get my fill of you while I can."

Iman wasn't about to point out that she offered to cancel her plans to see him later. Not when his long, muscled body was draped over hers and already grinding. Her legs encircled his waist, her hips falling into his rhythm. "Might as well."

Quickly grabbing a condom from the nightstand, Rasheed leaned back to cover himself before returning his body to Iman's, enjoying a few more of her kisses before trailing his tongue between her breasts to her toned stomach. He loved her body and how tight it was. And he loved how readily she gave herself over to him; she always wanted him as much as he wanted her, and showed it.

"You gon' make me late for work," she breathed, though she was clearly in no hurry to speed things along. She writhed as he licked her bellybutton, eyes squeezed shut in pleasure.

"I'd better make it worth it, then." Rasheed leaned up on his long arms, hovering over her as his eyes roamed her toffee-brown face. Their eyes locked together as he reached between them and slid inside of her, taking his time and enjoying the long groan that Iman released as he did so. They fell into a smooth pace, moving in tandem, his brown eyes fixed on hers.

"You feel *so* good..." He growled, briefly throwing his head back before returning his eyes to her. "Damn, Iman..."

"Yes..." Her hands slid up his chest before squeezing his shoulders. "God, yes, Rasheed."

They continued enjoying each other, the pace and intensity progressing from smooth and unhurried to jerky and frantic. Rasheed had Iman's legs bent back to her shoulders as he pounded into her, sweat dripping from his brow and a deep frown of concentration on his face.

"Come for me, Rasheed," she moaned. Her hand gripped his forearm. "'Cause I'm about to come for you."

"Shit!" Rasheed ground his hips against her, getting as deep as he could. He knew she loved that. Sure enough, it sent her over the edge and she was clawing at the pillows and the headboard, calling out his name and a string of colorful curses. Rasheed wasn't too far behind her with his release, gritting his teeth as he exploded inside of her, the condom catching everything he had.

After releasing her legs, he gently extracted then collapsed next to her, both of them panting and satisfied. Even though they both had places to be, neither seemed to care as they continued to lay there, enjoying being around each other.

"You know I'm gonna be thinking about that all day now, right?" Iman finally muttered, looking over at him with a smile.

He smiled back at her. "Good."

Iman didn't want to move, but knew she had to. As much as she would've loved to have laid there with Rasheed all day, she knew she couldn't afford to get fired because she was in a dick coma.

Reluctantly, she sat up and looked back at him. "I'll call you?"

He nodded. "Yeah."

Without another word, she pushed herself off the bed and strolled into the bathroom. Rasheed remained in bed, eying her naked body. He sighed and rubbed a hand down his face, scratching his slightly unkempt beard. He was still in the same spot when Iman emerged from the bathroom, showered and dressed, and came over to give him a quick kiss before scurrying out the door. Rasheed could still smell her pink sugar scent in the air.

Rasheed wasn't used to this. He'd had several casual relationships over the years and not once did he ever want them to be anything more than that. But with Iman, it felt different. They had agreed to keep things light, but that wasn't feeling like it was enough for him anymore. But he didn't want to break their groove by bringing it up; she might stop their arrangement altogether.

Knowing he couldn't lay around all day agonizing over it, he got up and got ready to get on with his day.

Several hours later, Iman almost tingled with excitement as she refreshed her lipstick in the rearview mirror of her car. She had pulled up to Rasheed's, anticipating his reaction upon seeing her. Charmaine had called a couple hours earlier, asking to reschedule their girls night out, and Iman was all too eager to agree. She hadn't wanted to cancel on her friend, and was thrilled that she didn't have to. Now she could spend the evening the way she really wanted to.

Rasheed had been on her mind all day. Their sex that morning had been amazing, but that was nothing new. Iman had more enjoyed just being around him, engaging in their effortless banter and teases and conversation. At some point, she had stopped looking at him as just her sex buddy and started looking at him as someone she could really fall for. He just made her feel...priceless.

She knew she couldn't tell him all this, though. They'd both agreed the night they first got drunk and she dared him to kiss her that they would keep things casual. She didn't want him thinking she was scheming this whole time, claiming to be down for one thing but really planning on something else. Catching feelings for Rasheed wasn't in her plans.

But hopefully, he would be happy to see her now. She'd started to call him after Charmaine cancelled on her but decided she wanted to surprise him. They'd exchanged a few texts throughout the day, and he mentioned something else about wishing he could see her later, but then quickly tacked an 'LOL' at the end of it. Well, he was about to get his wish.

Satisfied with her appearance, Iman grabbed her purse and got out of her car. She could hear the music coming from Rasheed's house and figured he was probably playing video games, something he liked to do to clear his mind after long days of working in a warehouse. She knocked on the door, the smile already on her lips.

"Come in!" Rasheed called out.

Iman quickly opened the door, her smile fading slightly. Rasheed wasn't alone. There were a few of his friends there, smoking and listening to music and playing cards.

But the one that caught Iman's attention was the woman that was sitting awfully close to Rasheed on the couch.

Rasheed's eyes were focused on the television screen as he played whatever version of Grand Theft Auto everyone was currently crazy about. He looked up and grinned when he saw Iman.

"Hey!" he greeted, though he made no move to stand. His eyes quickly shifted back to the game. "I thought you said you couldn't come by."

"Yeah, I know..." Iman glanced around the room, giving a halfhearted wave to his friends as they lifted their chins to her in acknowledgement. "There was a change in plans."

"Cool."

"I didn't mean to interrupt, though." She tried not to focus on the busty woman who was still squeezed next to Rasheed, even though there was plenty of room on the couch. And he didn't seem to mind her sitting so close; if he did, he surely would've let her know. Rasheed wasn't one to hold his tongue about much. "I can...go."

"You don't have to," Rasheed quickly retorted, looking up at her. "Stay and hang out. There's some pizza over there on the counter, if you want some."

Iman wanted Rasheed to put all these people out so they could be alone, but she knew she had no right to expect that. She *did* just show up unannounced. And just because she wanted to spend the evening cuddled up with him didn't mean he wanted the same thing.

And as she sat in the armchair one of his friends offered her, nibbling on the barely-warm slice of hamburger and pepper pizza, it became increasingly clear that he didn't. He barely paid her any attention. He just kept playing his stupid game, letting that woman in the ridiculously short shorts rub up against him. Iman watched as she whispered something in Rasheed's ear, earning a wide grin from him, then he whispered something back to her. When the girl placed her hand high on Rasheed's thigh, Iman felt her face tighten. Was he sleeping with her, too?

The thought upset her, and she knew she needed to get out of there before her cool façade cracked completely.

She got up to toss the rest of her pizza slice before going to use the bathroom, taking a moment to compose herself. Maybe this was just what she needed to see; proof that Rasheed wasn't interested in anything deep with her. It was a good thing she hadn't done anything foolish and told him about her growing feelings for him.

When she finally emerged from the bathroom, she jumped when she saw Rasheed standing there waiting for her.

"You good?" he asked her.

"Yeah." She forced a small smile. "I'm about to head out, though."

"Why?"

"It's just...I'm more tired than I thought I was. And you're clearly busy...no need in me hanging around here, being in the way. I'll just talk to you later."

Rasheed looked at her, itching to tell her that he didn't want her to go. He had only invited his friends over because Iman had said she couldn't come by and he wanted a distraction. They weren't even close friends; just some people he was cool with from work. But all Iman had to do was say the word and he'd put them all out.

But why would she say the word? That wasn't the kind of relationship they had.

"Can I at least have a kiss first?" he asked, stepping closer to her.

Iman glanced back towards the living room. "You sure that's a good idea?"

He frowned, confused. "Why wouldn't it be?"

She started to answer, but stopped herself. "Nothing; never mind." She leaned up and gave him a quick peck on the lips, placing her hand on his chest. "Call me tomorrow."

Then she turned and headed down the hallway to the living room. Rasheed could hear her saying goodbye to his guests, then the front door closed. He just slumped against the wall, running a hand over his low-cut black hair before dropping his head, looking at the floor.

Chapter 4

Lavinia & Ricky Hyman

Ricky trudged behind his wife through the furniture outlet, wishing he could be just about anywhere else.

"I cannot believe it's taking us this long to find another couch," Lavinia groused, absently running her hand along the back of a tan sectional. "It shouldn't be this hard."

"I've picked out at least five couches, Lavinia," Ricky pointed out.

"Yeah, but I didn't like any of those."

"And *I* don't love taking off work to go furniture shopping with you, either, but I compromise. I'm sure that's a foreign concept to you, though."

She whirled around, glaring at him. "You trying to be funny?"

"Not at all."

"Ricky, I really don't appreciate you getting an attitude just because I want to choose the right stuff for our house." She continued walking, expecting him to follow, which he did. "We both agreed to redecorate."

"But clearly we both don't get to decide on what we redecorate *with*, because you've shot down every suggestion I've had so far. Just like you didn't listen to me when it came to the renovations, going behind my back to the contractor and changing the plans because you decided it wasn't what *you* wanted."

"You said you were okay with that. That you were fine with whatever I decided."

"No I didn't, Lavinia. What I *said* was that I didn't care 'cause I was tired of arguing with you about it. You clearly were going to keep hounding me until you got your way. As usual."

"Ricky." She shook her head. "Stop tripping."

She stopped in front of a white leather couch, humming with intrigue. After a quick glance at the price tag, she dropped down onto it, running her hands over the material.

"I *really* like this one," she stated, grinning. She looked up at him. "What do you think?"

Ricky hated leather furniture, nor did he want a white couch, and Lavinia knew that. But he knew that didn't matter much to her. With a disinterested shrug, he droned, "I don't care."

Her shoulders slumped. "Ricky."

"What? We both know you don't give a damn what I think and are just gonna get what you want, anyway. So just buy the sofa so we can get outta here. I'm hungry."

"Well, I'm sorry; I thought you said you liked pleasing me. Happy wife, happy life, right?"

Resisting the urge to roll his eyes, Ricky just shook his head. He hated that stupid saying; it completely disregarded the husband. When did it become okay for everything to be about what the wife wanted?

Instead of acknowledging her question, he just asked, "You getting the sofa or not?"

"I'm not sure." She pursed her lips thoughtfully, tapping her nails on the cushion. "I don't think I'm in *love* with it, you know? I want to be in love with it."

"Let's go, then. We've been around this store twice already."

"I'm not ready yet. There are a couple more I want to look at again."

"Fine. I'll be in the car." He turned to leave.

"Wait!"

Sighing, he turned back to her. "What?"

"You're right; we can just go with this one." She popped up off the couch with a satisfied smile. "This will look great with the other stuff I picked out."

"Great."

After they found a salesperson, made the purchase and arranged for delivery, they finally left. Once they were in Ricky's Tahoe, Lavinia spoke up again.

"Don't forget, my mama is coming to stay with us for a while."

He looked at her in surprise before his expression melted into annoyance. He chuckled sarcastically. "How could I forget when you never told me that in the first place?"

"Yes, I did."

"No you didn't, Lavinia. I would've remembered that."

"Well, whatever. She's coming."

Ricky knew it was futile to try to argue. He didn't much care for Lavinia's mother and could only tolerate her in small doses. She was nosy and pushy, the latter trait she surely passed on to her only daughter. Lavinia was spoiled and used to getting her way, which Ricky had known when they were dating, but he didn't think she would morph into being selfish, too. But over the course of their eleven-year marriage, that's exactly what happened.

He hadn't been happy over their last couple of years together, and had begun just going through the motions with her without even realizing it. Part of him hoped things would get better, but the bigger part of him knew not to hold his breath. Lavinia wasn't going to change because she didn't think she ever did anything wrong.

"What does she need to say with us for?" he couldn't resist asking.

"She just needs a little break from Daddy. You know they butt heads a lot."

"I can relate."

"What?"

Ricky stayed silent, leaning farther away from her as he kept his eyes on the road.

"I really wish you wouldn't act like that, Ricky," Lavinia stated, her eyes boring into him. "You know Mama's been through a lot. She needs some attention. I'd think my husband would be willing to do whatever is necessary to help her feel better, just like I would. She's *your* family, too."

His jaw clenched, Ricky stayed quiet.

"I can't believe you're being this way. I thought you had my back. You know having my back means having my parents' back, too. Damn, I thought a husband was supposed to stand behind his wife."

His foot jammed down harder than necessary at the red light they pulled up to, causing Lavinia to lurch forward in her seat.

"It's funny how you wanna give me this speech about family and having folks' backs yet you insisted my dad stay in a hotel when he came to visit."

She sucked her teeth. "That's not the same thing. Your dad makes me uncomfortable. I always feel like he's looking at me too much."

"You feel like he does or he does?"

"Whatever. The fact that he makes me uncomfortable should be enough for you. Plus, I hate that cologne he always wears. I don't want my house smelling like that cheap stuff."

Breathe, man, he silently urged himself. Ricky knew he needed to calm down, because he was having visions of finding a sturdy tree to slam his passenger side into. It wasn't the first time thoughts like this entered his mind, and it freaked him out. He wasn't a violent man, but the more time he spent with his wife, the more his imagination ran wild. He had to ask himself, yet again, why he was staying with her.

"Don't forget, baby," she cooed, reaching over to place a hand on his thigh. He instantly stiffened. "Happy wife, happy life."

Ricky resisted the urge to push her hand off of him. He didn't trust himself not to say anything downright disrespectful, so he stayed quiet.

They didn't speak again for the rest of the day. That night, Ricky got out of bed after Lavinia fell asleep and went to the den to sleep on the couch.

The next day, Ricky still had no words for his wife as they prepared separate breakfasts and got ready for work. When Lavinia emerged from their walk-in closet in a top that showed way too much cleavage and an inappropriately-tight skirt, Ricky shook his head.

"How do I look?" she asked him, smiling proudly as she did a little turn for him.

"Why are you bothering to ask what I think? You're gonna wear it, regardless."

Her smile faded slightly. "What are you trying to say? You don't like it?"

"That outfit is totally inappropriate for work, Lavinia."

"Who says?"

"I'm the one you asked. But anybody with any sense would agree."

"Please. That's crazy."

"What's crazy is you thinking people aren't questioning your professionalism when you're always showing up wearing that kind of stuff. You don't think your real estate clients think some kind of way about that? What, you trying to entice people with your body?"

"No, but so what if I was? There's nothing wrong with using what I have to gain an advantage. And let's face it, clients are a lot more eager to cooperate if they like looking at what's sitting in front of them."

Ricky started to ask what else she was willing to do to *entice* her clients, but stopped himself. He didn't think he wanted to know.

"Like I said, you don't care what I say." He adjusted his tie and pulled his shoulder-length black locs into a low ponytail.

Lavinia eyed him. "You don't think I look good, baby?"

He just grunted. It wasn't like he was a robot; Lavinia might not have been high on his list of favorite people but he wasn't blind. The man in him still appreciated her voluptuous body, though he hadn't indulged in it in weeks. Dealing with her had gotten so bad lately that sex was the last thing on his mind most of the time. And on the nights he did need to release, he had two perfectly good hands.

When he didn't respond, she sauntered over to him, sliding her hands up his back before pressing her large breasts against it. She reached her hands around for his crotch, and when he started to move away, she yanked him back.

"We have some time," she informed in a low voice. "If you hate what I'm wearing, take it off of me."

Ricky willed his dick to calm down, though it wasn't exactly easy. Being so close to his luscious wife, feeling her body and smelling her sweet jasmine scent, caused latent parts of him to wake up against his will. His eyes fell to his watch and he knew he had time to bend her over if he wanted to, if only to release his own frustrations. It wouldn't be about making love. And really, Lavinia would likely prefer that, anyway, so she wouldn't have to worry about messing up her hair.

"Come on, you know you want this," Lavinia urged, giving his dick a teasing squeeze. She began softly grinding against him, her hand gripping his hip pulling him back against her in rhythm. "I haven't gotten any in too long. Give it to me, baby."

Ricky suddenly pushed her hands away, scurrying away from her and causing her to stumble back a couple of steps. She actually looked confused at the angry expression on his face.

"What's wrong with you?" she exclaimed.

"Last I checked, *I* was the one with the dick."

"What??"

"You're standing there grinding on me from behind like you're ready to bend me over the bed or something. I don't play that shit."

"Oh my god, are you serious??"

"Hell yeah, I'm serious."

"That is not what I was doing. I was just trying to be close to you. Since when did you get so paranoid? I thought you were secure in your masculinity."

"I'm plenty secure. That doesn't mean I'm gonna just allow shit I don't like."

"But you *should* like it."

"Why, because you say so?"

"Because I'm your wife. Hell, if I wanted to bring a strap-on into our bedroom-"

"You try that and your shit will be packed so fast it'll make your head spin." He looked at her with every ounce of seriousness in his body. "Do *not* try me, Lavinia."

His words seemed to humble her, and she almost looked timid. He couldn't deny he enjoyed her looking meek, especially since it didn't happen often. "I was just kidding, Ricky."

"Well, I'm not." He jammed his feet into his shoes and his wallet into his pocket. Any thoughts of indulging in his wife's body had gone up in smoke. Not even looking at her, he headed for the door. "I'm out."

"What time are you coming home?" she called out after him.

"When I'm done with everything I need to do. It'll be late."

"How late?"

"Late. Don't wait up."

"You remember about going to Taj and Serenity's tomorrow for game night, right?"

Ricky had temporarily forgotten about that, but was grateful for the reminder. It was finally something he could look forward to, besides getting away from Lavinia for the bulk of the day. Plus, he always enjoyed time with his friends.

"Yeah," was his simple reply, continuing out of the room and down the stairs. He grabbed his briefcase from beside the couch and headed outside.

Once inside his truck, he released a long, weary sigh, rubbing his eyes. He didn't know how things had gotten this bad. He never would've imagined that he'd have a marriage like this, where he didn't even like his wife most of the time and relished being away from her more than he did with her. His boy Taj suggested that he and Lavinia go to marriage counseling, which Ricky wasn't opposed to, but he knew Lavinia would scoff at it. She wouldn't want some therapist telling her what to do.

That didn't mean he couldn't go see one himself, though. He dialed his therapist's number, seeing if he could squeeze in a session after work.

Chapter 5

Serenity had been trying to think of a reason to cancel couple's night.

She loved hanging out with her friends, but the thought of Rasheed being in her house had her on edge. She'd given countless pep talks to herself to keep it together; they had an agreement. As long as he kept his mouth shut like he promised, she wouldn't have anything to worry about.

"You good, babe?" Taj asked her that morning, taking a bite of his avocado toast. "You've seemed on edge these past couple of days."

She avoided his eyes as she poured green tea into her insulated cup. "Just have a few things on my mind, that's all."

"Well, talk to me. Maybe I can help. It's been bugging you for a while, whatever it is."

"I appreciate it, sweetie, but it's just something I have to deal with on my own." She forced a smile and caressed the side of his face. "But I love you for wanting to be there for me."

"Absolutely." He leaned down to kiss her lips. "I don't like seeing you stressing."

"I know. I'll...I'll handle it. I'm sorry for being so distant lately."

"Yeah." Taj strummed his black suspenders with his thumb, eying the cuffs of his black trousers that stopped just above his ankles. He sipped his own green tea. "Especially last night."

Her face flamed. "I said I was sorry about that."

His eyes turned to her. "How much longer are we gonna keep doing this, Serenity?"

"Doing what?"

"Ignoring the huge elephant in the room. It's not healthy to keep acting like it isn't there."

"Taj..." She eased away from him to needlessly tighten the lid on her cup. "This is just a rough patch, if you can even call it that. We don't have a *real* problem. Believe me, there are couples who go through far more serious things than we do. Look at Lavinia and Ricky. Even Charmaine and Ace seem like they're on shaky ground, based on what she told me and Iman."

"And I feel for them but I'm more worried about *us*," Taj insisted. "I disagree that we don't have real problems. And we can't fix anything until we acknowledge that."

"Look, sweetie, I know I haven't been the most fun to live with lately, and I'm sorry for that; I appreciate you being so patient with me. But we don't need to invite any unnecessary drama into our relationship. And I don't want to bring other people into our business. Like I said, this is just a rough patch." She picked up her cup and the slice of avocado toast Taj had set aside for her. "It'll pass. We're fine."

Taj just eyed her. She could have this round, he decided. He was temporarily out of energy to get her to stop deluding herself and deal with what he knew she was as aware of as he was. They'd been tiptoeing around it for the past year.

"I've gotta go; those apple pies don't make themselves. They always sell out first at the café. Plus I have to make the ones for tonight, too," Serenity said, leaning up to give him a kiss. "I'll see you tonight."

"All right."

"I love you."

"Love you, too, babe."

He stood there leaning against the sink, watching her walk out and wishing he knew what to do to change what they both knew was wrong between them.

Sighing, he gulped the rest of his tea, quickly washed the dishes he used, and went to get started with his own work day.

Hours later, Serenity and Taj were both back home, straightening up before their friends arrived. Serenity was checking on the apple pies in the oven and arranging the other snacks she and Taj had prepared; a fruit and cheese tray, stuffed mushrooms, wings, and chips with pico de gallo. There were also several bottles of wine, apple cider (Charmaine's favorite), and bottles of water. Serenity hadn't been able to shake the nervousness for this evening. It remained in the back of her mind all through her work day. She knew she had to think positively; if she went into it paranoid, something was bound to happen.

Finally, the doorbell rang. When she opened the door and saw Iman standing there alone, her hopes shot up like a rocket.

"Hey, girl," she greeted, her eyes sweeping behind Iman. "You came by yourself?"

"Yep." Iman stepped inside and removed her jean jacket, revealing her cropped v-neck top and low-slung jeans. She'd never been shy about showing off her toned body.

Serenity gave her a hug. "Rasheed isn't coming?"

"Yeah, he is. We just didn't come together."

"Oh." Serenity tried not to look as disappointed as she felt. "Are you two okay? You were sounding kinda down when I talked to you the other day."

"Yeah, girl, I'm fine," Iman insisted a little too brightly. "Me and Rasheed are still just, you know...doing our thing, no strings attached."

Before Serenity could respond, Taj emerged from the back of the house. He smiled upon seeing Iman. "Hey there, pretty lady."

Iman grinned. "Hey Taj." They shared a friendly hug as the doorbell rang again.

As soon as Serenity opened the door, Charmaine bolted in and went straight to the kitchen. "I hope y'all have plenty of wine."

"What in the world..." Serenity marveled, turning questioning eyes to Ace, who just shrugged.

"You know how y'all women get when you're on your period," he commented.

The three ladies whipped around to glare at him, and Taj just shook his head. He should've known it wouldn't take long for Ace to put his foot in his mouth.

"What?" Ace asked, looking at all of them innocently.

"I am *not* on my period, Ace!" Charmaine snapped, filling a wineglass with chardonnay.

"And even if she was, that's not something you broadcast," Iman added, nudging him.

"Come on, we're all adults," Ace defended. "Everybody knows y'all have those. If it's not that, I don't know what it is, then; she's had an attitude for a couple of days now. I smell pie."

"Yeah, Serenity, it smells amazing in here," Iman added, moving over to the kitchen and peering through the window on the stove. "When are these things gonna be ready?"

"Just another couple of minutes," Serenity promised, glancing at her watch. "I made two of them this time; hopefully they'll last longer than they did last time we all hung out."

"You should've made one just for me, then, 'cause you know I go *in* on your pies," Ace joked.

Serenity forced a chuckle as everyone began helping themselves to the food. She wanted to ask Charmaine what was going on with her; the frown hadn't left her face since she walked through the door and she clearly was too agitated for just her usual cider. But Serenity knew that wasn't the time to get into it.

"I wonder where Ricky and Lavinia are," Taj commented, popping a mushroom cap into his mouth and looking at his watch. "They're running late."

"Maybe Ricky finally left her," Ace suggested, chuckling. "Or put her out."

Everyone looked at him.

"What?"

"Do you *ever* think before you speak?" Iman asked.

Charmaine snorted. "Of course not."

"Damn, where's y'all's sense of humor?" Ace grumbled, stuffing a pico de gallo-loaded chip into his mouth. "Y'all can never take a joke."

"It wasn't funny, man," Taj informed him. "Those are our friends you're talking about. Their marriage issues aren't something to clown about."

"It's not like I said I *want* it to happen," Ace defended. "But we all know Ricky isn't exactly living in wedded bliss over there."

"Yeah, well, regardless..."

There was a knock on the door before Rasheed let himself in. "Hey, people."

Serenity immediately tensed up and took a large gulp of her wine.

Everyone greeted him good-naturedly before he went around giving hugs and handshakes. When he got to Iman, he gave her a hesitant kiss on the cheek.

"Hey," he said in a lowered voice.

She looked up at him with a small smile. "Hey."

"Rasheed, have you heard from Ricky or Lavinia?" Taj asked him.

"Not really. But I do know they're outside in your driveway getting busy."

"What??" everyone screamed, rushing over to the windows. Ricky's Tahoe was parked behind Iman's Kia Sorrento. The windows were tinted but there was distinct rocking, and they could very faintly hear Lavinia's voice, urging Ricky on. Iman giggled.

"That's my boy!" Ace cheered, actually pumping his fist.

"Well, I guess they're not doing *too* bad," Serenity mused.

"I wonder how long they're gonna be out there," Charmaine mumbled. "And why they chose to do it in a driveway instead of at home."

"Hey, sometimes the urge hits and you just have to get it in right then and there," Iman responded. "For all we know, they did it before they left the house, too."

"Yeah, Lavinia *can* be a little greedy," Rasheed agreed. "Homegirl stays revved up."

"The fact that we know that is a little disturbing," Taj chuckled.

Serenity silently moved to the kitchen to remove the pies from the oven and take a breather. She jumped when she heard Rasheed's voice.

"Need some help?"

Keeping her eyes on what she was doing, Serenity shook her head. "No, thanks."

"You sure?" He moved closer to where she stood. "It's the least I could do."

"I'm good."

"You look nice."

She stiffened, finally looking at him. Glancing towards the living room, she went to stand in front of him, looking up into his handsome tawny brown, scruffy-bearded face.

"Remember, you promised," she reminded him in a hushed voice. "Please don't...you promised."

"I know, Serenity." He looked into her worried brown eyes that he always thought were pretty. He always thought *Serenity* was pretty. She was almost the opposite of Iman, who was tall and honey-skinned and brazenly sexy, with her black and grey braids and tight body; he considered Serenity just as attractive, though, with her rich chocolate brown skin that seemed to glow regardless of what light she was in, short natural hair, and gorgeous smile. And while her style tended to lean more towards flowy bohemian, she almost always wore off-the-shoulder shirts, giving a peek of that beautiful brown skin of hers. He hoped his boy Taj appreciated what he had.

"I said I wasn't gonna say anything, and I won't," he assured her, glancing behind him. He didn't want Iman hearing their conversation any more than Serenity wanted Taj hearing it. "I'm taking it to the grave, I told you that."

"I really hope you mean that, Rasheed." She rubbed a nervous hand down her arm. "It's hard enough being around you without looking suspicious."

"Hey, no need to be nervous around *me*." He arched a brow. "My part in all this is just a matter of bad timing. And Taj is my boy; it's not like I'm in any hurry to upset him."

"Thank you."

"Though you know stuff like this has a way of coming out at some point, right? I mean, secrets eventually make themselves known like worms out of dirt."

"I'll...tell him soon enough," Serenity insisted, ignoring Rasheed's skeptical look. Not that she could blame him, because she wasn't sure she was being totally honest, either. It had been a year and she still hadn't confessed yet. She knew it made her a coward, but she could admit to herself that she likely wouldn't admit anything to Taj until or unless she absolutely had to. "I just have to find the right time."

Rasheed didn't believe that and she knew it. He just grabbed a bottle of water and headed back to the living room.

Chapter 6

"We're trying to have a baby."

Everyone looked at Lavinia in shock. That was the last thing they'd expected to hear after she and Ricky finally came in from their driveway romp.

"Um, really?" Charmaine hedged. "That's a surprise."

"Yeah, it was a surprise to me, too," Ricky mumbled. "She neglected to mention that was the reason she jumped me until *after* we were done."

Lavinia nonchalantly reapplied her lipstick. "I knew if I did, you would've tried to say no."

"I wouldn't have *tried*. I *would* have said no."

"Well, there you go. That's why I didn't mention it."

"You're supposed to be on birth control."

"I quit taking that months ago. Surprise." She actually grinned and winked at him before turning her attention to her compact mirror, running her fingers through her expensive weave.

Ricky was giving his wife a look that sent a chill up Taj's spine, and he quickly went over to him and slung an arm around his shoulder.

"Let's take a walk, man," he suggested, pulling his friend away. Ricky wordlessly went along with him, glaring at Lavinia until he was out of the room.

"Lavinia, girl, that's messed up," Iman couldn't help commenting. "How are you gonna do Ricky like that?"

"What?" Lavinia looked genuinely confused. "You act like I tricked him or something."

"You did."

"This is the kind of stuff y'all women dog men for," Ace chimed in with a shake of his head. "No wonder he looked like he was ready to burn something down when he came in here."

"Ricky is my *husband*," Lavinia defended. "And he knows I'm ready to have kids."

"Not to gang up on you, Lavinia, but that's something you *both* have to want," Serenity commented.

"He does want it. He just doesn't know it yet. Once the baby is born, he'll fall in love with it just like I will."

They all looked at her like she was crazy.

"I'm gonna go make sure my boy is all right," Ace said, shaking his head again and heading in the direction Taj had led Ricky.

"Yeah, me, too." Rasheed followed him, sipping his water.

Lavinia snapped her compact closed and dropped it back into her purse. Serenity, Iman, and Charmaine were all still looking at her in disbelief.

"Stop it," Lavinia warned. "I don't need any lectures tonight. I'm hungry; where's the food?'

Knowing there was no talking any sense into her, her friends backed off. Lavinia was going to do what Lavinia wanted to do and was a master of justifying her actions, even if it made no sense to anyone else.

The ladies sat around eating and chatting. It was a good twenty minutes before the men came back in, with Ricky only looking marginally less angry than before. Lavinia scooted over on the couch to make room for him, but he dropped into the chair that Taj had brought in from the kitchen. Lavinia looked momentarily shocked, but quickly recovered.

"So, what games are we playing?" she asked, a little louder than necessary.

"I have a fun one for us to do after we eat," Taj announced, smiling. He wanted to lighten some of the tension in the air. "It should be really interesting."

"What, it's a secret?" Ace asked, amused, as he filled his plastic plate with wings.

"Ehh. Not really. I just wanted it to be something other than just us playing spades or dominos or watching movies like we usually do."

"So this'll be less drama than that, then?" Iman asked. "'Cause you know somebody always gets to fussing when we play spades."

Taj shrugged. "It might be different drama, if not less."

"You surely have me curious now."

"Yeah, so let's hurry up and eat so we can get to it."

"This isn't gonna involve some kind of physical activity, like charades or something like that, is it?" Charmaine asked. "I'm not sure I'm up for trying to act out movie titles."

Taj shook his head. "It's not charades."

"Is this a thing where you're gonna start out with some kind of game and then really spring a surprise proposal on Serenity?" Ace excitedly inquired. "That would be kinda dope."

"It would be shot to hell now if it was, huh?"

"You can still do it. Y'all have been together forever."

Taj shot a pensive glance at Serenity, who looked at him evenly. He began to wonder if she was waiting for a proposal. They'd talked about marriage a few times over their relationship, and at one time he was sure he wanted to ask her to be his wife, but his enthusiasm about that had slowed over recent months. He felt they had some issues they needed to deal with before taking that step.

Serenity wanted to marry Taj with everything in her, but she knew she'd have to come clean with him about some things before she could accept a proposal from him in good conscience. These were things she hadn't even told her girls about. It was too embarrassing. But she knew the time would come when she'd have to stop pretending like she and Taj were perfect.

The friends continued to eat and chat about what was going on with their respective careers and other random things before Taj decided to get things kicked off. He knew there would be some resistance once everyone learned what he had planned for the night, but he hoped they'd open their minds to it.

"So this is what I wanted us to get into tonight," he announced, after making a quick trip his bedroom. He held up a deck of cards.

"I thought you said we weren't playing cards," Rasheed noted.

"I said we weren't playing *spades*," Taj verified. "This is a relationship question-and-answer game."

He could almost feel the vibe shift in the room. A couple of his friends' facial expressions went from curious to nervous immediately.

"Like trivia?" Lavinia asked.

"Not really. It's more like questions that are designed to stimulate conversation; see how well we know each other. It can even make us closer, if we're all honest with our answers."

"Or it can open up huge cans of worms we might not be ready for," Ace muttered.

Charmaine's head snapped to him. "You got something to hide?"

"I just don't think we need to know every little thing about each other. There are some things we *should* keep to ourselves. Hell, I probably wouldn't like half the people I know if I knew more about them."

Her face tightened. Now she was curious as to just what Ace was keeping from her. "I'm in, Taj."

"Me too," Lavinia chimed in. "I'm an open book."

Ricky just grunted, resting his jaw on his fist. He looked like he'd rather be anywhere else.

"What the hell," Rasheed shrugged.

"Yeah, let's do it," Iman added. "I'm always ready to get in folks' business."

Taj looked at Serenity, who was fumbling with her fingers in her lap. "What about you, baby?"

She wanted to say no. She had no idea this was what Taj had been planning, or she would've tried to talk him out of it. This was the last thing she wanted to participate in.

But if she said that, she'd have to say why. And she knew a simple *I'd rather not* wouldn't be good enough for her friends. And Taj would surely get suspicious.

"That's fine," she made herself say, forcing a smile. "Should be fun."

"Ricky?" Taj asked.

Shrugging, Ricky reached for the last stuffed mushroom on his plate. "Whatever."

All eyes turned to Ace. He acted like he didn't see everyone looking at him, taking his time chugging the last of his apple cider. He licked his thick lips and pointed to the fruit and cheese tray, which was now almost empty. "I never thought I'd like strawberries and cheese together but it ain't half bad. Charmaine, babe, we should have that at our reception. Is that brie?"

"Dammit, Ace!" Lavinia huffed, frowning and placing a fist on her thick hip. "We don't have all night."

"Fine," Ace conceded with a shrug. "But don't say I didn't warn y'all."

Serenity dared to glance at Rasheed and quickly looked away when she found him already eyeing her. Dread was coursing through her so hard it almost made her fidgety. Why did Taj have to suggest this??

But she told herself it might not be so bad. Maybe the questions were of the tame variety, like describing an ideal date or where a dream vacation would be. She couldn't imagine Taj would suggest a game that could cause any kind of dissention among their friends, or within his relationship with her.

It'll be fine, she silently assured.

"All right, then," Taj grinned, tossing the box of cards between this hands. Serenity hadn't seen him look that excited in a while. "Let's get it going."

Since the game wasn't exactly meant to be played by eight people at once, Taj produced a spinner to help determine who would pose questions to whom, instead of just having everyone take turns asking things to their respective partners.

"That should make things more interesting," he explained, re-taking his seat.

"Oh, I think this will be plenty interesting as it is," Iman joked, tucking her leg underneath her. She grinned at Rasheed, who was sitting next to her. "I can't wait to hear what questions *you* get asked."

"Me, either," Rasheed chuckled. He inched a little closer to her, making a move to put his arm around her before abruptly stopping, as if catching himself.

"Before we kick this off, y'all, I think it goes without saying that there's no point in doing this if everyone isn't gonna be honest," Taj declared, looking around at everyone. "It's supposed to be fun but it's also supposed to help us all get to know each other better; get deeper insight to one another. We can't do that if people are gonna hold back or not be straight up."

Everyone agreed, some more enthusiastically than others.

Taj shuffled the cards before putting them in a stack by the spinner on the coffee table. "So we'll just take turns spinning and whoever it lands on, you pick a card from the deck and ask them the question. Simple."

"Let's get it going, then," Rasheed exclaimed with a loud clap of his hands.

"I'll spin first," Taj offered. He paused in reaching for the spinner, glancing around. "Unless someone else wants to."

"I'll go," Ace quickly offered, sitting forward in one of the wooden kitchen table chairs that Taj had brought in. "The more I'm asking the questions, the less I'm answering 'em."

They went through a few rounds of questions that, to Serenity's relief, were rather tame. But she should've known that it would only be a matter of time before things kicked up a notch.

When it was Ace's turn to spin again, he said, "I know I wasn't hyped about playing this, but it's pretty cool, learning more about y'all like this. Are there any more challenging questions in here, though, Taj?"

"Just keep drawing, man."

A couple of people chuckled. Ace sat forward, playfully rubbing his hands together before thumping the spinner, sending it whirling. Everyone leaned forward to see where it would land, and there were some chuckles and some sighs of relief when it landed on Lavinia.

Ace grinned. "It almost don't even matter what I ask; this should be good." He eagerly pulled a card from the top of the deck and cleared his throat. "Do you think it's okay if a woman makes more money than her boyfriend or husband?"

"Of course it is!" Lavinia wasted no time answering. "A woman shouldn't have to feel guilty about any success she earned just because her man would be all tucked in the balls about it. His insecurity and issues are *his* business. As long as he's making money, too, why should it matter, anyway?"

"I can feel you on that, girl," Iman cosigned.

"But as for me and *my* house," Lavinia couldn't resist adding, "I wouldn't be all the way thrilled with it if I was bringing in loaves while my husband only brought in crumbs. If Ricky didn't make more than me, I don't even know if we'd be married right now."

That emitted various reactions, from gasps to grunts. Everyone's eyes slid over to Ricky, whose gaze was fixated on Lavinia. He didn't look angry, but he certainly didn't look pleased, either.

"Is that right?" he asked her, his voice even.

"This isn't news. You know how I personally think the man should make more than the woman."

"I didn't know our marriage hinged on who made the most."

"That's not what I said."

"Yes, it is."

"I see we're coming in hot," Rasheed muttered.

"At least things are getting put out on the table," Taj reasoned. "Lavinia, you spin next."

She tore her glare from Ricky to flick the spinner, smiling when it landed on Iman. She quickly drew a card. "When is the last time you've had a crush?"

Her face flushing immediately, Iman sat up a little straighter. She looked uncharacteristically nervous. "Umm...I couldn't even say."

"What you mean, you couldn't say?" Ace pressed.

Iman's eyes flicked to Rasheed, who seemed very interested in her answer with the way he was sitting forward, looking at her. Even though everyone knew they were sleeping together, she wasn't planning on letting him know she had an actual crush on him just yet. She didn't want him thinking she was trying to take things deeper than they agreed. "I mean I'm not sure. It's not like I keep track of that."

"I thought we were supposed to be honest," Ricky spoke up. "Iman, if you want to know our business, we need to know yours. We all know you've had a damn crush, if you don't have one now. Your face got as red as those strawberries when he asked you that."

"Ugh, fine," Iman sighed, dropping her hands beside her. "I guess you could say I have a crush on somebody."

"Who?" Lavinia persisted.

"The question didn't say *who*. It said *when*," Iman quickly averted, holding up a finger. "So my answer is I have a crush on somebody now. That's the end of the answer. Now, my turn." She willed her face to stop flaming as she moved to flick the spinner, feeling Rasheed's eyes still on her. She would've given anything to have been able to read his mind right then. Was he upset?

The spinner landed on Taj. Iman drew a card. "On a scale of one to ten, how important do you think sex is in a relationship?"

Pursing his lips, Taj appeared thoughtful, nodding his head. It didn't take him long to think about it. "Nine."

"Nine?" Serenity placed a hand on his arm. "That high?"

Taj just looked at her and shrugged. "It's a pretty big deal. I know its PC to say that sex shouldn't matter but it does. What, you disagree?"

"I mean...it matters but I don't know if I'd put it at a *nine*. There are more important things to focus on when two people love each other."

"Serenity, girl, stop acting like you don't enjoy getting it in just like anybody else," Lavina joked. "You might come across tame but you're probably an animal behind closed doors."

"Lavinia!" Serenity's face was flaming, hating that several pairs of intrigued eyes were on her. "Can we not?"

Iman sucked her teeth. "I don't know why you're acting all shy. We're all friends here. And grown. It's no secret that we all enjoy sex."

"I know *you* do," Rasheed whispered in her ear. Iman just grinned and playfully bumped his shoulder.

"Yeah, but enjoying it and actually *getting* it are two different things," Taj muttered, earning a gasp from Serenity.

"Don't tell me you're holding out on your man," Lavinia barked at Serenity, who was still gaping at Taj. "Girl, that's a no-no. You should *stay* hot and ready. Trust, I know what it's like to walk around horny all the damn time 'cause your partner is being selfish."

"So I guess that's why you resorted to trickery, huh?" Ricky immediately countered. "And why would I wanna smash when we hardly get along half the time?"

"Hell, I'll take the angry sex. It's better than nothing."

"Whatever."

"Taj and I are just fine in the bedroom," Serenity hastily insisted, holding up her hands.

"Not what it seems like from here," Rasheed noted. Serenity glared at him.

Taj looked like he wanted to say something but stopped himself. "Anyway. Next." He flicked the spinner and it landed on Charmaine. Taj took a card.

"At what percentage would you say your current happiness level is in your relationship?"

"Hmph," Charmaine immediately scoffed. She glared at Ace, her arms tightly folded and crossed leg rapidly swinging back and forth. "*Maybe* fifty-five. Sixty on a good day."

"What??" Ace exclaimed incredulously, shooting forward in his chair. "That's it? You're actually trying to say you're not happy with me? How come you never said anything about that before now?"

"Maybe I didn't think you would hear me if I did. You only listen if you feel like it."

"Huh?? What have I not listened to you about?"

Charmaine's eyes tightened. "How about this stupid waffle restaurant idea you keep spouting all over the place? As if you have any business trying to run a restaurant. Not to mention, when it fails, you'd be pulling *me* down right along with you!"

Ace looked absolutely stung. He clearly had no idea she felt this way. "You could've told me that before."

"I told you when you first started talking about it that I didn't think it was the best idea. And when I tried to tell you why, you cut me off. You didn't give a damn *what* I thought; you were gonna do what you wanted to do."

"Damn, girl, if I knew that all it would take was you getting slithered for you to speak your mind, I'd have liquored you up months ago," Iman muttered, eying Charmaine as she chugged the rest of her wine.

"Oh, so you've been telling your girls you're not cool with me but kept *me* in the dark, huh?" Ace surmised accusingly to his fuming fiancée. "That's real nice, considering how much you're always talking about how important communication and all that shit is."

Charmaine rolled her eyes. "Shut up, Ace."

"Shut up??"

"Yes, *shut up.*"

"How are you gonna tell me to-"

"Y'all, come on," Taj interjected, holding out his arms as he looked back and forth between them. "Let's not let our emotions get the best of us, here."

"Easy for you to say. *Your* woman didn't just tell the world she hates you."

"Ugh, that's *not* what she said, Ace," Lavinia groaned, exasperated. "You're so damn dramatic. And this is clearly what she's talking about; you don't listen."

Ricky almost laughed out loud. "And the pot calls the kettle..."

"Excuse me??"

"Charmaine, it's your turn," Serenity quickly spoke up as Lavinia and Ricky looked like they were about to face off. "Hopefully you'll draw a more lighthearted question."

"Hmph." Charmaine sat forward and thumped the spinner so hard that it flew off the coffee table. After Taj picked it up and placed it back in front of her, she told herself to calm down as she thumped it again with less force. It landed on Rasheed, and Serenity suddenly picked up her wine glass.

"This oughta be good," Iman grinned as Charmaine snatched up a card.

Charmaine cut her eyes at Ace before turning to face Rasheed, the card held up in front of her face. "All right, Rasheed...do you think that sex ruins friendships?"

Rasheed paused. "That's what it really says?"

"Yeah..."

"Oh. No, sex doesn't have to *ruin* friendships, even if it changes 'em. As long as everybody is straight up about what they're feeling, it's all good."

"So you're being *straight up* with Iman, then, huh?" Ace challenged, his arms tightly folded.

Feeling Iman's curious eyes on him, Rasheed resisted the urge to throw something at his friend. He knew he shouldn't have told Ace about his growing feelings for Iman. "That wasn't the question."

"Is there something you need to tell me, Rasheed?" Iman asked him.

"No. There is not."

"Sounds like there is."

"Iman..."

"You might as well go on and tell her, man," Ace spoke up again. "Y'all wanted to do all this opening up and shit. Now is as good a time as any."

"Shut up, Ace."

"I'm about tired of y'all telling me to shut up."

"Quit talking so much, then." Rasheed glanced at Iman, who was still eying him as if she expected an explanation. "There's nothing to tell. You know not to listen to Ace."

"What??"

"So you're trying to say you never told him anything about you and me?" Iman pressed, sitting up straighter. "I know how y'all guys talk. What did you say about me, Rasheed?"

"Can we not do this now?" Rasheed hissed, finally turning to look at her. "I really don't think now is the time to be talking about our...whatever it is we're doing."

"Our...relationship?"

Rasheed bit his lip. "Is that what you call it?"

They stared at each other for a few moments before Iman sank back in her seat. "Maybe I shouldn't."

"Spin the damn thing, man," Ricky said to Rasheed. "Y'all can keep avoiding how you feel about each other another day."

Finally tearing his eyes from Iman, Rasheed reached forward to thump the spinner. Everything in him wished the two of them were alone, because his curiosity about Iman's comment was through the roof. Did she want an actual relationship with him or was she just saying that because they were in front of everybody? Now he wondered what she talked about when it was just her and the women; Rasheed surely was regretting confiding in Ace, he knew that.

When the spinner landed on Serenity, Rasheed drew a card and distractedly read, "How many secrets have you kept from your partner over the course of your relationship?"

The color seemed to drain from Serenity's face. It was on the tip of her tongue to ask Rasheed to choose another card but she knew that would be like throwing herself right under the bus. She'd only kept one secret from Taj but it was a big one.

"Umm..." she hedged, chuckling nervously. "Who *hasn't* kept a secret from their partner, huh? My mother had a secret savings account that she kept from my dad for years. And Dad would sneak out of the house to eat steak after she refused to have red meat in the house anymore."

"That's all fascinating but that doesn't have anything to do with you and Taj," Lavinia pointed out. "You are stalling, girl."

"I'm *not* stalling," Serenity countered, cutting her eyes at her friend.

"What, you have some secrets you don't want me to know about, babe?" Taj asked her, a playful tilt to his voice though his eyes were full of apprehension.

"Umm...I guess you could say I've kept something from you since we got together," Serenity made herself admit. "But it's...I personally think a little mystery in a relationship is a good thing. I'm sure there are things that you've kept from me, right?"

Taj pursed his lips, his eyes roaming her face thoughtfully. "Yeah, actually."

She blinked as a couple of gasps went up around the room. "Really? You...have secrets from me, Taj?"

He took his time reaching for his glass of wine before slowly taking a long swallow. "I do. Been keeping it for a while, too."

"Wh-what is it?"

He shook his head. "I don't think you can handle hearing it in front of everybody."

Serenity glanced around before looking back at him. "It's that bad?"

Taj turned and gave her a challenging look. "I'll tell you mine if you tell me yours."

"Awww shit..." Ace muttered.

Serenity held Taj's look before sinking against the back of the couch. "Maybe you're right; it can wait."

"You might as well spill it. It's just gonna haunt you both since you know there are secrets now," Lavinia suggested. "Ricky and I might not be perfect but we don't have any secrets."

"Hmph," Ace scoffed, while Rasheed cleared his throat. Lavinia looked at them both before looking back at Ricky.

"What?"

Ricky shrugged. "I don't tell you everything, Lavinia."

She frowned. "And just what haven't you told me?"

"Plenty of stuff."

"Like??"

"Oh, let's see...how 'bout how I don't want to have a child with you. Why would I want a baby with a wife I don't even like coming home to half the time? I work late so much by design, not necessity. You've made me miserable in my own damn house. And before you try to ask why I never said anything before now, I've tried to talk to you about how unhappy I was getting, but you either always make the conversation about you or brush off whatever concerns I have. So..." He leaned back in his chair, looking like a weight had been lifted. "There it is."

The room was quiet as everyone sat there in shock. Even though Ricky had confided in the men about his unhappiness in his marriage, even they didn't know just how deep it ran. And they certainly never expected him to just blurt it out in front of everyone like that.

Lavinia was beside herself. Part of her thought Ricky was just trying to get a rise out of her, but the bigger part knew better. Her face burned with hurt and embarrassment. "Oh, so it's like that? Well...it's not like you're the only one that's unhappy, you know. Before tonight, you've been all stingy with the dick and I'm tired of it. It's been getting old having to use my damn vibrators so much when I have a fine husband right in the house. Maybe that's why I let it happen when my coworker kissed me last year."

"Oooh!" Iman hooted.

"*Hell* no!" Ace yelled, glaring at Lavinia while Ricky remained unfazed. "How are you gonna do my boy like that!"

"You don't have any room to be talking, Mr. Jackrabbit," Charmaine snapped at him. "You might not be *stingy with the dick*, as she put it, but you don't know the first damn thing about making love or being intimate."

Ace's frown deepened. "So you're just gonna keep calling me out, huh? If you're still mad about me missing the cake tasting, just say that, but you ain't gotta-"

"*Yes*, I'm still mad about that, you idiot!" Charmaine screamed, shooting out of her chair. "I'm mad about that and a lot of other stuff! And maybe I'm worried about us ending up like *them*!" She pointed her fingers at Lavinia and Ricky.

"Like us??" Lavinia was clearly offended.

"Yeah, you *should* be," Ricky said to Charmaine, standing from his chair. "Because we're damn sure not anything to emulate. I'm telling you, Charmaine, if you're this unhappy *now*, you might need to reconsider whether you need to be getting married or not."

"Ricky, what the hell, man?" Ace demanded.

"Hey, I'm just sayin'."

"At least it seems like Ace likes being with you sexually, Charmaine," Taj couldn't resist chiming in. "Because *I* certainly can't relate lately."

Serenity's head whipped around to him as her face flamed in alarm. "Taj!"

"What? This clearly is how I need to get it out, since you refuse to talk about it any other time. You want to keep acting like we're good when we're not. I love you, Serenity, but there's a reason I haven't proposed to you yet."

More gasps were heard. Taj's face was pinched in a frown, glaring at his girlfriend.

Serenity started to place a hand on his shoulder but stopped herself. Clearing her throat, she muttered, "I thought we agreed-"

"We didn't agree to anything. You wanted to keep sweeping everything under the rug and hope our problems would just melt into the ground but it doesn't work like that. We can't fix stuff we won't touch. And you never wanting to give as good as you get in the bedroom is a problem. I've been sexually frustrated for too long and I'm over it."

Serenity itched to run out of the room. The last thing she wanted was for everyone to know about their sexual issues.

"I told you I was sorry about that-"

"Yeah, you keep saying you're sorry," Taj snapped. "But want you *won't* say is why you switched up and got like that in the first place. Because up until about a year ago, you weren't like this. So something must have happened for things to change like they have."

Serenity's eyes darted towards Rasheed all on their own before flitting to Ace, then Charmaine, then Ricky, then Iman. She was looking at everyone but Taj. Of course she'd known he was unhappy with their sex life and had noticed the change in her; he wasn't an idiot. But she had no idea how deep his frustration ran since he'd been so patient with her. He was a patient man, in general. But she should've known it would only be a matter of time before that patience ran out.

"I, um...Taj, sweetie, I know there are some things I need to explain to you-"

"Does you clamping it up in the bedroom have anything to do with the secret you're keeping from Taj?" Lavinia interjected, being rewarded with an instant glare from Serenity.

"Is there any more wine?" Ace loudly inquired.

"It...does have something to do with someone in this room," Serenity hesitantly admitted. "But I'd rather tell Taj the details in private."

"Oh, now you wanna get tight-lipped after you've heard all of our business," Ricky scoffed with a shake of the head. "Whatever. I'm over this, anyway. I'm going to the bathroom."

"Yeah, let's put a pause on this so we can cool out," Rasheed suggested as Ricky stalked out of the room. "I think enough has been said for one night."

"Yeah, thanks a lot, Taj," Ace grumbled. "This was a *great* idea, to cause drama in all of our relationships."

"I'm *glad* I got that stuff off my chest," Charmaine countered, glaring at him as she stood from her chair. "Iman, girl, I appreciate you staying on me about telling him the real deal. I should've done it months ago."

"Oh, so you can tell her what to do in *her* relationship but you can't tell Rasheed-"

"Be quiet, Lavinia," Iman cut her off. "Like Rasheed said, enough has been said for tonight."

"Don't be co-signing with him now like he's your man."

Iman glared at her while Serenity dared to look over at Taj. His hard eyes were already on her and her throat immediately went dry. Now that he knew she was keeping something from him, she felt immense pressure to finally tell him what had been weighing on her for the past year. But she didn't know how in the world she was going to do it.

Then there was a loud door slam and everyone's heads whipped around.

"What was that?" Charmaine asked.

Taj stood and went to the front door, with Rasheed on his heels. They each took a peek out of one of the windows flanking the front door and gave a pensive glance towards each other.

"What's wrong?" Serenity asked, noticing their expressions.

"Umm," Rasheed scratched the back of his neck. "Lavinia, you might need to call a rideshare."

"What??" Lavinia screeched, shooting off the couch and making a beeline for the door. She bumped Taj out of the way and yanked the front door open, her jaw dropping when she saw Ricky's Tahoe missing from the driveway. "He actually *left* me?!"

"Lavinia, girl, I'll give you a ride," Iman offered. "I think it's safe to say this evening is a wrap. I'm gonna go home and drink some hard liquor. Might even dip into my edibles after all this."

"I hope you're planning on sharing 'cause I'm staying with you tonight." Lavinia folded her arms under her large breasts in a huff. "I'm damn sure not going home to Ricky after he left me hanging like this. And don't none of ya'll tell him where I am, either. Let him worry."

"You *do* remember him saying he didn't like it when you were there anyway, right?"

"Shut up, Ace!" everyone yelled.

"Man, forget this," Ace mumbled, plunking his glass on the coffee table so hard it cracked. He just sucked his teeth and stood. "Come on, Charmaine, let's get up outta here."

"I'm going to Iman's, too," Charmaine announced defiantly.

"Excuse me? So not only do you spend most of the night dogging me, now you're not even coming home??"

"I think we need a break from each other for a minute. I'm gonna have to think about some things, Ace."

"Like what?" The concern in Ace's frown was unmistakable. He grabbed her wrist as she tried to walk past him. "What are you saying?"

She looked into his eyes as if seeing him for the first time. "I said what I said, Ace. I just need a minute."

Pulling her wrist from his grasp, she grabbed her purse and headed towards the door, filing out after Lavinia. Iman and Rasheed shared a look before she walked out after them, and he stood there watching as the three of them piled into her car and took off.

In the next few minutes, Ace and Rasheed left, also, and Serenity and Taj just looked at each other.

"Well," Taj spoke when it was clear she wasn't going to, "Isn't there something you need to tell me?"

Chapter 7

Lavinia & Ricky

It was a couple of days before Lavinia went back home. She stayed at Iman's, constantly checking her phone for a message from Ricky asking where she was or telling her she needed to come home so they could talk. But he never sent anything.

She managed to convince herself that one of their friends told him her whereabouts and that's why he hadn't reached out. Once he had some time to cool off, he'd be thinking rationally again. There must have been some things going on at work or something causing him to be so irritable, which had to be the only reason he said the things he said to her at couple's night. There was no way he could have meant any of that. Lavinia knew their relationship wasn't perfect, but it wasn't as bad as Ricky had made it seem.

Instead of calling him to let him know she was on the way home, she decided to just show up so he wouldn't try to make himself scarce. When she entered the house and heard Ricky upstairs moving around, she smiled, knowing he would be glad to see her.

But Ricky's expression was anything but happy when Lavinia strutted into their bedroom. He just glanced up at her before returning his eyes to the book he was holding with a disappointed grunt.

Lavinia waited for him to speak to her. After several moments of no acknowledgment, she sighed. "Ricky."

His jaw automatically tightened. "What?"

"How come I didn't hear from you these past couple days?"

"Hear from me for what?"

"To make sure I was okay, maybe? Your wife doesn't come home and you don't even call?"

"Ace already told me where you were, not that I asked. And let's not act like my calling would've made any difference. You were clearly trying to prove something, so..."

"So? Damn, Ricky, you act like you don't care if I come back here or not."

Ricky finally looked back up at her with empty eyes. Lavinia remembered when he used to look at her with love and desire and compassion; now, he might as well have been looking at a stranger.

"I think you've made it very clear you're all about what you want," he finally grumbled. "Even if I *had* gone over to Iman's to bring you back here, you would've tried to show me up and punish me in front of your friends for the stuff I said the other night, trying to teach me some kind of lesson. And I'm sure you're gonna try to deny that, but whatever." He closed his book and stood from the bed. "I'm not trying to waste any more energy on fights I can't win with you."

"So what does that mean?" Lavinia trailed him as he padded into their walk-in closet. "What are you trying to say, Ricky?"

He shot her an irritated glance. "Why are you following me?"

"We need to talk."

"No we don't."

"Look, if you're mad about what I said about the kiss with my coworker...it didn't mean anything. Marshawn has had a crush on me for years and we had a few too many drinks at that office party you didn't want to go to, and it just happened. I told him it couldn't happen again."

"Uh-huh." Ricky grabbed a pair of Jordans from his shoe rack and brushed past her.

She was right on his heels. "I'm serious, Ricky. Regardless of whatever issues we have, you're still the only man I want."

"As long as I do whatever you want and give in to your every wish, right?" He sat on the bed to put on his sneakers.

"No!"

"See, I don't even know what the point of us talking is if we're not gonna be straight up. You know good and damn well you want everything to be your way or no way, going around spouting that 'happy wife, happy life' bullshit and throwing a tantrum whenever I dare to tell you no. You're selfish."

"I just know what I want and I go for it. If that makes me selfish-"

"And you twist everything to accommodate you, not to mention how you can never admit when you're wrong." He stood. "And I'm over it."

Her eyes widened. "Are you trying to tell me you're leaving me?"

"It's crossed my mind," he responded without hesitation.

Feeling like the wind had gotten knocked out of her, Lavinia placed a hand to her chest and stepped back. She never thought she'd hear Ricky say those words to her. What happened to 'for better or for worse'?

"I thought a husband was supposed to stick with his wife through the tough times," she finally accused. "We have some issues and you just give up?"

He chuckled sarcastically, running a hand through his locs. "*Both* of us have to be willing to work on things, Lavinia. And really, it's only because of my therapist that I'm even still here. If I hadn't started seeing them to learn how to deal with my anger and frustration towards you, I'd have been outta here months ago."

Lavinia recoiled. "*Therapist*? Since when did you start seeing a therapist?"

"Big surprise that's the part you focus on. A while ago."

"What's 'a while'?"

"Does it matter?" he snapped, frustrated. "I'm seeing one. That's it."

"What's their name? I don't like this, Ricky. No husband of mine needs to be seeing a damn therapist, especially if all you're doing is complaining about me. Do you know how weak that makes you look?"

Ricky wondered how weak she'd think he was if he slapped her so hard her wig flew off, and he made himself count to ten and take a deep breath, just like Dr. Morrow had instructed when he had such thoughts. Despite how much Lavinia pissed him off, he didn't want to put his hands on her. That wasn't the kind of man he was, and it still freaked him out that those kinds of thoughts even entered his mind, and with increasing frequency.

Knowing he needed to get away from her, Ricky grabbed his keys from the dresser. "I'm out."

"Where are you going? We're not done with this."

"Yeah, we are."

"You were just in here reading a minute ago and now that I'm here, you wanna run off. You're always running."

"You're always giving me reason to." He headed for the door.

"Ricky. Ricky!"

Just over the threshold, he reluctantly stopped and turned his head in her direction.

"You need to stop seeing that doctor," Lavinia ordered strongly. "We can work out our own problems."

"*You're* my damn problem, Lavinia. What part of that don't you *get*??" He looked right into her eyes. "I told you, I wouldn't even still be here if it wasn't for my going to those sessions. It's the only way I can tolerate your ass! And maybe if you weren't so worried about what folks are gonna think and would admit you're part in all this, we'd be a lot better off!"

Despite herself, tears sprang to Lavinia's eyes. Ricky was acting like he didn't even like her, let alone love her anymore. And this was one time she wasn't able to conjure an argument to convince herself otherwise.

"Fine, then. Just go," she muttered, storming into their en suite bathroom and slamming the door. Ricky turned and left without another word.

Very few words were spoken in the Hyman household over the next few days. Ricky continued to delay going home as much as he could, either by staying at work late or hanging out with the fellas. And when he finally did go home, he purposely avoided his wife as much as possible. They hadn't slept in the same bed in weeks.

Lavinia hated all the tension in her house but she was determined not to be the one to break. To her, Ricky was blowing things out of proportion. She tried to be a good wife to him, keeping her hair and nails done and her body tight. Not that any of that mattered, since he barely touched her. Their romp in Taj and Serenity's driveway was the first time they'd had sex in months. And since her pregnancy tests kept coming back negative, her spontaneous seduction hadn't even worked. She'd been hoping that she was knocked up; Ricky would surely soften towards her if he knew she was carrying his baby. He loved kids and talked a lot about being a father early in their relationship. Lavinia hadn't been ready then, and in truth, she still wasn't, but desperate times called for desperate measures.

She didn't know how she was going to get Ricky back into their bed, though. He was intent on staying away from her. Wouldn't even grace her with a 'good morning' let alone make love to her. She couldn't even remember the last time they kissed; the sex in his Tahoe had been straight to the point with no foreplay.

It still burned her that Ricky was seeing a therapist. More notably, that he was going to someone else just to vent about her. He made it seem like she was the most terrible person on the planet, when in actuality she was just self-assured and decisive. How was that a bad thing? And why did he even marry her in the first place if he didn't like the kind of woman she was?

Thank goodness her mother was coming. There needed to be something in the house to break up the tension. And if it couldn't be a baby, her mother Darla was the next best thing.

Unfortunately, Ricky didn't agree. He'd forgotten all about Darla's impending visit and when she and Lavinia walked into the house late one morning as he was in the kitchen eating breakfast, he groaned out loud.

"Baby, look who's here!" Lavinia greeted with a grin as she and Darla entered the room, trying to silently send him the message to at least act glad to see her mother.

Ricky either missed the message or ignored it because he was anything but. "Dammit."

"Ricky!"

"Not glad to see me, huh?" Darla surmised with a smirk.

"No offense, Ms. Darla, but now really isn't the ideal time for houseguests," Ricky stated, stuffing the last of his sausage and egg sandwich into his mouth.

"Oh yeah? Why not?"

He took a long sip of his coffee. "It just isn't."

"Well, I certainly don't wanna impose on you two-"

"What? No, don't listen to him, Mama," Lavinia quickly interjected. "There's nothing wrong with you being here now. Ricky is just a little cranky, that's all."

"Tough times at work?" Darla asked Ricky, who was putting his plate in the sink. "You do something with computers, right?"

Ricky drained his coffee before putting the cup in the sink on top of the plate. "I'm an IT consultant. And work isn't my problem." He eyed his wife.

Lavinia's face tightened as she returned his glare, but she quickly forced a smile. "Let's get your things up to the guest room, Mama."

She turned and scurried out of the room, with Darla following her after throwing a curious glance towards Ricky, who stood there fuming. Once again, Lavinia had totally disregarded his wishes. He didn't know what made her think they needed someone else in their house when they were going through what they were. The last thing Ricky needed was a double-team.

He was grateful that he had a session scheduled with Dr. Morrow later, because he surely needed it. It was taking everything in him not to go right upstairs and pack a bag so he could go to a hotel; if Darla was at his house, he didn't want to be. It would just be days of her and Lavinia cackling and making jokes at his expense and basically taking over the house. He didn't need to be there for that.

Feeling his ire rising, he grabbed the edge of the quartz countertop and closed his eyes, counting to ten. Then he took several deep breaths, conjuring up a pleasant memory like Dr. Morrow suggested. Surprisingly, his mind went to his and Lavinia's wedding day. He'd been so excited to make her his wife; the grin never left his face as she strode down the aisle in her body-hugging lace wedding gown. In that moment, he wasn't kicking himself for giving in to Lavinia and spending way more money on their wedding than he wanted to. He rationalized that she deserved that indulgence.

The last thing he expected was for her headstrong nature to snowball into outright selfishness and entitlement.

His brow furrowed. He hated that things had gotten this bad. Never in a million years would he have thought that he'd be in the position where he didn't even like being around his wife. What he felt for Lavinia now was a far cry from what he felt for her when he was waiting for her at the altar.

With a tired sigh, he tried to find a bright side to Darla being there. At least maybe Lavinia would be too occupied entertaining her mother to bother him. It wasn't like they included him in their plans. That used to bug him but he was grateful for it now.

Then he heard Dr. Morrow's voice in his head telling him to try to make an effort to make peace. That if he tried to let go of some of his anger and make a sincere go at saving his marriage, Lavinia would take his concerns more seriously and not think he was just lashing out.

It couldn't hurt, he figured. It wasn't like he didn't still love his wife, even if he didn't like her much lately. And he wanted it to be said that he did whatever he could to make things better.

With renewed resolve, Ricky headed for the stairs. He went over his words in his head, reminding himself to be calm and extend the proverbial olive branch. The stubborn part of him hated being the one to make the first move again, but if being the bigger person would bring some peace to his house, then he could suck it up and do it.

He heard his wife and mother-in-law before he got to the second floor landing, and was still too caught up in his own jumbled thoughts to register what they were saying. But as he continued down the hall towards the guest bedroom, he started paying attention:

"What is going on with you two?" Darla was asking in a somewhat-hushed voice.

"It's a mess around here," Lavinia replied with a dramatic sigh. Ricky noticed she wasn't trying to be as discreet as her mother. "Ricky has been tripping so hard lately, Mama. You wouldn't believe some of the things he's said to me."

"That bad?"

"Worse. He just walks around with an attitude all the time, mad at the world."

"Why, though? I can't imagine he's doing that for no reason."

There was a pause. "I think he just likes being mad," Lavinia responded, her voice slightly lowered. "All I ever do is try to make him happy, improve our home and be a good wife. He won't even give me the baby I've been asking for."

"Maybe he's cheating on you," Darla suggested. "Sometimes men start trying to do things to push the wife away when they've met someone else they think they wanna be with."

Ricky's face contorted, incredulous. What the hell? Despite whatever problems he and Lavinia had, he'd never stepped out on her or even thought about it. He wasn't a cheater. He'd just divorce her before doing that.

"It wouldn't surprise me, honestly," Lavinia responded easily, to Ricky's amazement. "He never seems to want to come home. No man stays at work or hangs with his boys *that* much. It sure would explain a lot."

"So what are you gonna do about it?"

"All men slip up eventually, so if he's cheating, I'll find out sooner or later. But really, Mama, I think he's just jealous that my career is going better than his. He's successful but it's taken him longer to move up the career ladder than its taking me. Hell, I'm the top seller in my office four months running. Between that and the fact that he probably knows he hasn't been satisfying me sexually lately, his self-esteem is in the toilet and he's lashing out at me because of it. That's why I'm being so patient with him. Some men just need that extra coddling."

"Hmm."

"You know he started seeing a therapist? My husband...my sexy, Black, supposedly-strong husband is actually seeing a shrink, *voluntarily*. But with all those issues, I guess I can see why."

"Not a lot of women would put up with all that, at least not without getting the attention they're lacking at home somewhere else. Or have you? It'll be our little secret if you did."

"I've *never* stepped out on Ricky. Never," Lavinia protested strongly. "Men push up on me all the time but I've never touched another man. Just because my husband is probably doing dirt doesn't mean I have to be wrong, too. No, I'm gonna stick by him through this phase he's going through. Once he finally gets it through his head that I have his back unconditionally, he'll stop treating me like the enemy and appreciate me more."

"So you're just sticking by your man and being patient."

"It's just what a good wife does."

Ricky didn't even realize he'd ripped a hole in his own sleeve until he looked down. The fact that his wife was standing in their house straight lying on him made him want to explode.

It was classic Lavinia; playing the victim and taking no ownership for her part in things.

He felt stupid for even considering trying to work things out with her. Her words were already replaying in his head and the more they did, the angrier he became. He knew he needed to get out of that house before he totally lost it and did something he would regret.

Not even bothering to pack anything, Ricky turned on his heel and headed downstairs for the door. He'd just buy whatever he needed. He couldn't be in the same house with his wife and her lies anymore.

As he jumped into his truck and peeled out of the driveway, he realized he needed to seriously consider if he wanted to still be Lavinia's husband. He never believed in running for divorce court at the first sign of trouble, but he also wasn't trying to look up years down the line and realize he was even more miserable than he was then, not to mention bitter. Life was just too short.

Telling himself he'd bring it up to Dr. Morrow later, he headed for the hotel, knowing he'd likely be there a while.

Chapter 8

Iman & Rasheed

"How long have you been banging Serenity?"

Rasheed's head whipped around. "What??"

"Don't play, Rasheed. I know something is going on between you two. I saw the looks she kept sneaking at you, looking guilty as hell." Iman shifted her weight to one side, placing a hand on her hip as she glared at her lover. "So I guess *you're* the reason she and Taj are having issues."

"Iman, you're not even close. I've never once touched Serenity like that."

She wasn't convinced. "*Something* happened. I saw how uncomfortable she got when you showed up at couple's night. In fact, I've noticed that she gets all squirrely around you a lot lately. You can't tell me there's no reason for that."

"There *is* a reason. Serenity is definitely keeping something from Taj but it's not about me."

"Then what is it about?"

"I can't tell you all that, Iman."

"Why can't you?"

"Because it's not my business to tell. Honestly, I'm surprised you don't know, since y'all ladies like to tell each other everything."

"Hmph." Iman's skeptical expression slowly faded as she stood there looking at him. She was relieved to hear that Rasheed wasn't messing around with Serenity. Ever since couple's night, it had bothered Iman that she and her girl were possibly sleeping with the same man at the same time. Iman was willing to do and try a lot of things, but sharing men wasn't one of them.

"You believe me, right?" Rasheed gently took the hand that was on her hip and played with her soft fingers. His brown eyes searched hers. "I'd never do no shit like that. Taj is my boy; it's bad enough I know about it and he doesn't."

"And I guess Serenity still hasn't said anything, since all hell hasn't broken loose. 'Cause I'm guessing it's a big deal, whatever it is."

"Yeah. It is." He pulled her into his arms. "But I don't wanna talk about them no more. I finally have you all to myself."

Iman moaned as Rasheed began slowly kissing and licking her neck. Her hands slid up his back and her eyes fluttered closed, leaning her head back to give him better access. What he was doing felt amazing and she tried to just surrender to the moment and enjoy it, but there was something else on her mind that she couldn't let go of.

Just as she was about to speak, though, Rasheed straightened and planted a deep, hard kiss to her lips, grunting his desire. Iman's arms automatically wrapped around his neck when he picked her up and headed to the bedroom. She stayed clamped onto him as he laid on her on his bed.

"Rasheed," she whispered, biting her lip as he licked a trail between her breasts. She felt they needed to talk but what he was doing felt too good to stop him. "Fuck..."

"Mmm-hmm..." His hands grabbed the waistband of her leggings and pulled. "Tell me you like it."

She squirmed under his tongue. "I like it."

Yanking her leggings all the way off and throwing them over his shoulder, he licked up the inside of her long leg until he got to what he'd been missing for days. They both moaned, loving it. "You missed me, Iman?"

"Yes..." Her hand grabbed his head, sliding her fingertips through his messy tapered 'fro. She liked that he was letting his hair grow out. "Hell yeah, I missed you."

"I missed you, too." He pushed her legs up. "Keep these out of my way so I can show you how much."

All thoughts flew out of Iman's mind as Rasheed proceeded to feast on her, enjoying it just as much as she was. He didn't know when, but he had gotten hooked on Iman's body and pleasuring it. He loved making her writhe and cuss and scream. And lately he'd been wanting her even more often.

He had no idea how mutual that feeling was. Iman realized she hated being away from Rasheed. Everything in her wanted to let him know that, but she kept losing her nerve. Even though she had the feeling that she wasn't alone in her growing feelings, she still couldn't bring herself to broach the subject and risk messing up what they had going.

"That's what I wanted," Rasheed declared after he'd made Iman climax so hard she almost choked him with her thighs. He stood, pulling his shirt over his head. "Now get naked."

Still panting and tingling from her orgasm, Iman felt her buzz intensify as she eyed Rasheed's bare chest. In the next moment, they were both ripping off the rest of their clothes and diving for each other.

"Damn, Iman," Rasheed growled, gripping her hips as he stroked her from the back. He gritted his teeth when she began throwing it back at him like he liked it. It felt so good he would've cried if it wouldn't have made him feel like such a chump. "Shit, I love…"

Iman looked over her shoulder at him but his eyes were squeezed shut. She wondered what the rest of that sentence was.

"Sit down, baby, I wanna ride you," she told him, easing to her stomach before rolling over. Once he was positioned with his back against the padded headboard, Iman straddled his lap, wasting no time rejoining them together. They held each other tightly, Rasheed's tongue on her breasts as she wound her narrow hips on him.

"I don't see myself ever getting tired of this," Rasheed muttered, looking up at her with half-lidded eyes. His arms tightened around her. "You've got me hooked, girl."

Iman gazed down at him, wondering if this was the opening she'd been waiting for. Maybe Rasheed wanted the same thing she did; for them to make this thing between them official.

"I'm hooked on you, too," she whispered.

They shared a look before Rasheed pulled her closer, burying his face between her breasts. They continued to please each other, each knowing this time was different but neither of them saying it.

Once they were spent and tangled in each other's arms, Iman rubbed her hand up and down Rasheed's chest, enjoying the post-sex scent of him. She closed her eyes and took a deep breath, telling herself to stop being a punk.

"Rasheed," she began, "There's something I think we should talk about."

"What's up?"

"This thing we're doing. Are you...satisfied with it?"

He took a beat before responding. "What you mean?"

"I mean...well, let me ask you this." She leaned back slightly to look at him. "Are you seeing anybody else?"

Another pause. "I'm surprised you would ask me that."

"Is that a yes or a no?"

"I'm not."

"For real?"

"Why do you sound surprised?"

"That night I came over after Charmaine canceled on me and all those people were over here..." She rested her head against his chest again. "That woman was sitting all up on you on the sofa and you two looked like...well, she looked like more than just a friend."

"That was just Kyra."

"And who is Kyra?"

"Just a woman at my job. We're not kicking it like that."

"She looked awfully flirty with you..."

"She's a flirt." He shrugged.

"...And you didn't seem to mind."

"I was barely paying her any attention, Iman. She was drunk, plus she flirts with damn near anything with a dick."

"Would you have felt some kind of way if you saw me hugged up with another dude like that?"

His arms tensed around her. "Probably."

"So..." She trailed a nail around his pec. "What does that mean?"

She could tell he was looking down at her but she kept her head in place. "Is there something you want it to mean, Iman?"

Steeling herself, Iman pulled back to look up at him. "Rasheed, at couple's night, what were the guys talking about with all that stuff they were saying about your feelings for me? For whatever reason, you didn't want to talk about it then."

"If I tell you that, will you tell me who it is you have a crush on?" His eyes roamed her still slightly-flushed face. "Because you weren't eager to talk about that, either."

"You think you're ready for the answer to that?"

They shared a long look. "Are you?" he retorted.

"If you're feeling differently about us and what we have going on, I wish you'd just say so, Rasheed."

"That doesn't just apply to me. Hell, if you're getting down with me while you're crushing on somebody else, I'd like to know that shit, too."

"Even though we said in the beginning that this was no strings and the only thing we cared about was what we did with each other? What happened to that?"

"Don't try to bring that up when you were just questioning me about Kyra a minute ago. If you can ask me about her, I can ask who else you're fucking, too, Iman!"

"I'm not fucking anybody else!"

Their staredown continued until both of them rolled onto their backs, as if on cue.

"We said we were gonna keep things light," Rasheed muttered with a sigh, rubbing his eyes.

Iman stared at the ceiling. "Yeah, we did."

"Is it me or does this not feel all that *light* anymore?"

"No." She sighed. "It's not just you. I think that ship sailed a while ago, and we need to deal with it."

"Yeah. We do."

"Are you spending the night?"

Rasheed wanted to, but his body seemed to sit up all on its own. The thought of Iman possibly telling him something he wouldn't want to hear made him retreat, even if it was just delaying the inevitable. "I want to but I have a stupid-early shift tomorrow. And we both know I can hardly resist you in the morning so I should probably head out. I'll call you, though."

Iman stayed quiet as she watched Rasheed get dressed, plant a soft kiss to her lips and then walk out the door. Rolling over to her side, she couldn't decide if she was finally making some progress with Rasheed or just wasting her time.

Chapter 9

Serenity & Taj

Serenity never thought she'd get to where she avoided going home. Once upon a time, she rushed home to be with Taj. But things hadn't been the same between them since couple's night.

Especially since she had stood in his face and lied to him. After everyone left and he all but demanded that she tell him what it was she'd been keeping from him, she lost her nerve and mumbled something about getting drunk with Lavinia one night and them sharing a one-time sexual experience together, which was a complete lie. She'd never touched Lavinia or any other woman sexually and had no desire to. But telling him that was easier than telling him what she really did.

"So...the reason you've been so stingy in the bedroom is because you and Lavinia sucked each other's breasts when you were drunk?"

Serenity averted her eyes, already hating that she'd even put that out there. She'd never been a very good liar. Even if she managed to say it, the guilt from lying always clawed at her until she confessed. She wasn't able to just go on about her business as if nothing happened, like the other party in her transgression seemed to be able to do.

Her face on fire, Serenity muttered, "Something like that."

"And, what, your guilt keeps you from pleasuring me like I pleasure you?"

"Yes..."

"It's not like I'm thrilled to hear about this, Serenity, but this is something you could've told me by now. You fooling around with your homegirl when you were drunk isn't the end of the world."

Serenity hated herself for lying to Taj again. He deserved to know what really happened. Maybe she should've told him when their friends were still there, so she'd have a buffer. Them being there alone was sucking all of her nerve. She was simply terrified how he'd respond.

"I...I guess I was embarrassed," she managed to say. "I'd never done anything like that before, and it was hard enough being around Lavinia afterwards. She, um, assured me it was just a one-time drunken thing that meant nothing and we should just forget about it."

"Okay, so why didn't you tell me then?"

"I was embarrassed, Taj, I told you. Even after Lavinia and I dealt with it, I still didn't know how to come clean about it to you. The fact that I'd been with someone else sexually, drunk or not...especially since it was one of our friends..."

"I get it, Serenity, but still. It's been over a year. And we've been together over *three* years. I'd like to think you could come to me about difficult stuff by now. If you can't, then what kind of relationship do we really even have?"

Everything in Serenity screamed to just fess up. She was only making things worse with this ridiculous lie. But she punked out as she'd done so many times since she betrayed the love of her life.

"You're right," she admitted, daring to look at him. He was so good to her, and she knew that he was probably at the end of his patience. A lot of men would have left her already, after how she'd been acting. She hadn't cut sex with Taj totally off, but she allowed him to do all kinds of things to her body while refusing to do much of anything to his. It wasn't fair and she knew it. But every time she tried to make herself touch Taj, she got a flashback to another brown male body in a hotel bed with her, and it extinguished any desire she had. "I know we can't keep going like this."

"So what are we gonna do about it? Now that you've confessed this, are you going to loosen up so we can go back to how we used to be?"

She knew that wasn't possible but she also knew that she couldn't tell him no. Now that she had dug the hole deeper for herself, she was going to have to find a way to get past her sexual block.

"Of course," she managed with a tight smile.

As she expected, Taj wasted no time testing her. As soon as they climbed into bed that night, he pulled her to him and laid a deep, intense kiss on her. His hand squeezed and kneaded her breast for a few moments before he rolled onto his back, looking at her with expectant eyes.

Knowing there was no backing out, Serenity made herself slowly kiss her way down his bare chest, somewhat hating that he'd come to bed already naked. His erection was already jockeying for her attention, and Serenity tried to clear her mind of everything else as she wrapped her hand around it and nervously licked her lips.

Leaning up on his elbows, Taj watched her intently. "Feels good to have your hands on me again."

Serenity responded by giving a few light licks to the head of his shaft before sliding her lips over it. Taj shuddered as his head fell back.

"Ahhh..."

Closing her eyes, Serenity tried to get into it, sucking the head as she knew he liked. His hand drifted into her short hair as he began thrusting his hips upward, trying to get further into her mouth. But Serenity's lips stayed clamped where they were, going no further down his long shaft like she knew he wanted her to.

"Take more of it in there, baby," he urged in a desperate whisper. It had been so long since she'd gone down on him and he was eager to get the full experience. "Come on, suck it how you know I like it."

Serenity tried to oblige, taking more of him into her mouth, even though she felt like she was going to throw up. Not because of Taj, but because of the mental images that she couldn't keep from flashing through her mind. *He* hadn't been able to get enough of her that night in that hotel room. She'd sucked more dick that night than she ever had in her life, and while she'd enjoyed making him lose his mind at the time, it rendered her unable to pleasure her man now.

Taj wasn't making it any easier for her, wanting her to go all in. Serenity should've known that he wouldn't be satisfied with a little teasing. After so many months of holding out, he was trying to make up for lost time. He'd want her to suck him until he came, preferably all over her bare breasts, before getting on top of him and riding him. He loved the reverse cowgirl position. Serenity used to love it, too.

His hips started pumping a little faster. "Go deeper, baby. Why you acting scared of it?"

Serenity *was* scared, and it was keeping her from being able to do what Taj wanted her to do. From what she *wanted* to do for him. She hated depriving him like she had been, especially since he hadn't been depriving her. If only she could just turn her mind off or block what happened out of it, she'd be able to give Taj the pleasure and release he deserved. But she couldn't.

He gripped her hair and tried to guide her mouth down deeper onto his dick, and Serenity immediately gagged.

"You okay?" Taj asked, looking at her with concern.

"Mmm-hmm." Gathering herself, Serenity tried again, opting to start again with just licking the head. She wished she could get away with keeping it at that. But before too long, there went Taj trying to push himself into her mouth again, whispering how bad he needed it. Serenity gripped the base and dove in, managing to get most of him into her mouth before she began coughing, feeling like she was about to choke.

"Just relax, babe," he urged, his grip on her hair tightening. He could feel her trying to retreat. "You know what I like. I miss how you used to go down on me; I need it. Come on, give it to me like that. Let loose, babe. It's just you and me."

It's just you and me. The same words *he* said that night when she was worried they were getting too loud in the hotel room.

She pushed back, firmly extracting his hand from her hair and sitting up on her knees. Tossing the covers over his dick so she wouldn't have to look at it, she covered her face with her hands as shameful tears began stinging her eyes.

"I'm so sorry," she cried from behind her hands. "I can't do this, I'm sorry."

She knew he was looking at her and could only imagine how frustrated he probably was. "What's the problem, Serenity? Is there something else going on that I don't know about? You're acting like you're being tortured or something."

"I...it's not that. I just...please give me a little more time. I'll do better but I need some more time."

"Time for *what*?" he snapped. "What the hell is wrong with you??"

Instead of answering, she just slid off the bed and scurried to the bathroom, slamming the door behind her. She stayed in there for almost two hours, ignoring his requests for her to come out and talk to him. Eventually, he left her alone. Serenity could hear him jacking off through the door, and her humiliation only got worse. When the room went quiet and Serenity peeked around the bathroom door and saw he was asleep with his back to her, she tiptoed past him and went to the living room, curling up on the couch as if she didn't deserve to even sleep in the same bed with him.

Things had been incredibly awkward between them since that night. They both avoided each other, taking their time going home and when they were there together, staying in separate parts of the house. They spoke to each other only when they needed to. And even when Serenity returned to their bed, they stayed as far away from each other as possible.

Serenity hated this. Every time he'd brush by her in the morning, barely mumbling a 'hello' before he headed out the door, it wrenched her heart. He wasn't even making breakfast for her anymore like he usually did, since he got up before her to do his yoga. Now, he just fended for himself. They didn't share meals, they didn't talk, they didn't touch. Serenity was grateful that he was even still coming home.

And every time she heard him masturbating in the shower or from across the bed or - as she discovered when she peeked out the window after he'd gotten home one night - in his car, it was like a punch to the chest. She knew he was taunting her, because he wasn't trying to be discreet. He'd get loud where he knew she could hear him, reminding him of what he had to do for himself because she refused to. Serenity just prayed she could get it together before he reached his breaking point.

Wanting to start getting them at least back on speaking terms, Serenity eased up behind him as he stood at the kitchen counter one morning, stirring agave into his steel cut oatmeal. She hated how he immediately tensed when she slid her hands up his back.

"Good morning, handsome," she greeted with a nervous bite of her lip.

He grunted. "Morning."

"Do you think you could sneak away and come to the café for lunch today?"

In no hurry to respond, he reached for the slivered almonds that were next to him and dumped them onto his oatmeal, taking his time stirring them in. "I don't know."

"I'd love it if you could. It's been a while since we've had lunch together."

"It's been a while since we've done *a few* things together," he retorted, turning to cut his eyes at her.

Serenity's shoulders slumped. "Taj, please..."

"I'm not sure I'd be very good company. I've been a little on edge, for obvious reasons." He picked up his bowl and stepped away from her touch. "When you're able to help me do something about that, or *really* tell me why you can't, then maybe we can talk."

"Okay, I guess that's fair, but..." She looked at him pleadingly. "Please know that I hate this as much as you do."

"Oh, I doubt that. Because you haven't been the one getting jipped for months on end. I've been giving you orgasms and pleasure on the regular and all I get is left hanging. So if we're talking about whose more frustrated, I'd win that easily."

"Baby-"

"I have to go, Serenity." He started to head out of the room.

"You haven't even finished your breakfast."

"I'll take it with me."

Sighing in defeat, Serenity decided to let it go. She knew nothing short of dropping to her knees in front of him would make things any better right then.

"I'll probably be home late tonight," she informed him before he left the kitchen. "Someone rented the café for a birthday party."

"Yeah." He grabbed his brown leather satchel from the couch, slung it across his shoulders, and stalked out without giving her another look. Serenity blinked back tears as she headed back to the bedroom to finish getting ready for the day.

It was tortuous being at work when all she could think about was Taj and the precarious state of their relationship. She knew that with every day that passed without her telling him the truth, she was just pushing him further away. The last thing she wanted was to lose Taj; he meant everything to her. That night she'd stepped out on him meant absolutely nothing, other than to cement that Taj was the only man for her. As soon as it was over, she knew she'd made a major mistake, and now the memory of it was punishing her.

She couldn't even explain why she'd done it; she hadn't been unhappy with Taj at all. There hadn't been anything missing from their relationship. Serenity knew without a doubt that she wanted to be Mrs. Taj Wharton. But one night of acting outside of herself would likely cost her that. Even if she finally managed to tell him everything, he'd probably still leave her because she waited so long to admit it, not to mention that she'd done it in the first place.

Serenity stood behind the counter at her café, mindlessly wiping it down as she eyed the woman whose birthday was being celebrated grinning and crying as she hugged her family, thanks to her boyfriend having just proposed to her. Serenity forced a pained smile as she watched the scene play out in front of her, wishing she could retreat to the back. Watching someone else get what she wanted for herself was yet another reminder that she needed to woman up and come clean with Taj.

When things were finally winding down, she left hasty instructions to her employees to get everything cleaned up and closed down, saying there was something urgent she had to go handle. As hard as it would be, she needed to finally tell Taj everything.

She stopped on the way home to get some Grey Goose, immediately breaking into it as soon as she pulled into her driveway. She needed the liquid courage. After a few gulps and a few deep breaths, she got out of the car and headed into the house, determined. Part of her was terrified of what might come of it, but the majority of her was eager to unburden herself of this secret she'd been carrying for too long.

The living room and kitchen were dark and empty, so Serenity headed back to their bedroom. She knew Taj was home because his Volkswagon was in the driveway. Her mind was so jumbled with what she was going to say that she didn't notice the moans until she got closer to her closed bedroom door.

Light escaped from underneath the door into the dark hallway, and Serenity felt a cold wave wash over her as she inched closer. Taj's moans were unmistakable but normal; it was the woman's voice that had Serenity's heart feel like it was about to explode out of her chest.

She could hear movement on the bed, and clamped a hand over her mouth. Was this really happening? Had Taj really brought another woman into their house? Into their *bed*? Serenity couldn't believe it had come to this. At least when she did her dirt, she did it in a hotel.

Her hand moved to open the door, but of course it was locked. Her fist raised to bang on the door, but the blinding tears weakened her. Hearing Taj moan about how good it felt sent Serenity running for the front door. As soon as she was back in her car, she pulled out her phone and made a call.

Chapter 10

Charmaine & Ace

"Charmaine, what is the big damn deal? I said I was sorry."

"That doesn't mean anything if you keep doing it, Ace."

"So I drank all the juice. Is that really worth getting so pissed about?"

"You drunk all the juice *and* left the empty jug in the refrigerator. Inconsiderate, as usual."

He shook his head. "I don't know what's up with you but you've been blowing off the handle at the most insignificant shit lately and I'm tired of it."

"Oh well, because I've been tired of a lot more than that."

"Is this still about the restaurant? I told you I'd press pause on that."

"Yeah, you said that. But then I heard you on the phone with Ricky talking about how you were still tweaking your business plan. Doesn't sound like 'pressing pause' to me."

Ace averted his eyes. "Babe-"

"Leave me alone, Ace."

They'd been arguing more and more since couple's night. Charmaine was finally speaking her mind about what frustrated her instead of letting it go like she'd made a habit of doing throughout their relationship, and it resulted in them butting heads more than ever. Ace was frustrated but he was also floored; he'd never seen his Charmaine like this. She'd always been so easygoing but now she was sounding off over the tiniest things.

Ace still blamed Taj. If he hadn't suggested that stupid game, he and Charmaine would still be happy and getting ready for their wedding instead of fussing about empty juice cartons.

"Charmaine," Ace hedged, entering the bedroom where she'd retreated to. He hated when they argued and just wanted to get back to how they were before. His brows lifted slightly when he noticed her getting off a call. "Who was that?"

"Serenity. She asked if she could come over."

He paused. "For what?"

"I don't know, but she was pretty upset. I think something happened with her and Taj."

"Oh. I'll be sure to leave you two alone." Coming up behind her as she stood at the dresser angrily rummaging through one of the drawers, he wrapped his arms around her, gently grabbing her wrists. "Can you please stop being mad at me?"

She sucked her teeth. "Why?"

"Why? Because we've been fussing way too much lately. We've barely even talked about the wedding recently at all."

Her tense body loosened slightly. "I know, Ace."

"So..." He turned her around to face him, lifting her chin and waiting for her to look at him. "Let's get back to that."

She looked at him for a long moment, her brown eyes thoughtful. "Ace..."

He leaned in and pressed his lips to hers. "Yeah?"

"I think we need to pull back a little bit. Or as you put it, *press pause*."

"On what?"

"On this." She held up her left hand, waving her round-cut diamond engagement ring in his face. She'd loved it when he presented it to her and asked her to be his wife, but now she had to make herself keep it on every day. "I don't think we're ready to get married."

Frowning, he dropped his arms and stepped back. "Are you kidding me with this?"

"No, Ace, I'm not."

"So now all of a sudden, you don't even wanna get married?"

"I didn't say I didn't want to *at all*. Just that we should hold off on it."

"For *no* reason."

"I gave you a reason."

"*I'm* ready to get married, Charmaine. My feelings for you haven't changed at all. You're the one who's switching stuff up."

"Dammit, Ace," Charmaine sighed, running her hands through her thin hair, "You can't keep sticking your head in the sand and ignoring what's happening. Can't you tell I've been unhappy? Does that not matter to you?"

"Of course it does. I've been trying to *make* you happy but you always start complaining about everything I do. Hell, if anybody needs to be trying to pull back, it's me, with the way you've been getting onto me about every damn thing."

She folded her arms. "Well, why haven't you, then?"

"Because *I* don't fall apart just because shit isn't perfect," he shot back at her. "So we argue sometimes, so what? What couple doesn't? It's nothing to freak out about."

"You still don't get it. Of course I know couples fight. But it's what we're fighting *about*. At the end of the day, Ace, you're still too thoughtless to be anybody's husband. And I don't want to end up resenting you because I just went along with it because you wanted me to. I've done too much of that, which I admit is part of the reason I'm so frustrated now. I've held my tongue way too much and let too much go."

"So I'm just that bad, huh? I've been *that* awful to you that now you're questioning everything about me and us?"

"That's not what I said."

"Maybe *I* need to rethink some shit too, then," Ace countered. "'Cause if this is how you're gonna overreact to every little thing-"

"See, this is what I'm talking about!" Charmaine exclaimed, shaking an extended hand towards him. "You keep making light of my feelings! It's not..." She sighed, suddenly drained. "This just isn't working."

He just stared at her. "I want it to, though."

"But it isn't." She looked away, shaking her head. "Look, Ace...I love you. But we're gonna need to make some changes...go to counseling or take some marriage classes or *something* if you want us to keep this going."

He laughed loudly, causing Charmaine's frown to deepen. "Marriage classes? Are you kidding me?"

"Do I look like I'm kidding, Ace?"

"That's ridiculous!"

Her expression hardened. "You can think it's ridiculous all you want to. You'd better hear what I'm saying. If we *don't* do something, if you don't fix your shit, we're *done*!"

His smile faded as she stomped out of the room, hearing the front door slam moments later. Ace couldn't believe this. How had things between them gotten this bad??

He trudged to the bed and flopped onto it, rubbing his eyes before staring blankly up at the ceiling. He'd wanted Charmaine ever since he first saw her at the grocery store four years earlier. She thought he was funny and agreed to hang out, but only as friends. She didn't take him seriously when he kept insisting that he was interested in her romantically. It took some serious pursuing to get her to agree to go on an actual date with him. And once she did, he vowed to never let her go. He knew when they went bowling and she beat him two games in a row and he didn't even care that he was a goner.

Ace was the first to admit that he wasn't perfect. He'd made plenty of mistakes throughout their relationship. But he never meant any harm. And he certainly didn't think it was anything they couldn't work through. Really, he felt a little foolish because the whole time he'd been thinking there wasn't anything that could come between him and Charmaine, she was stewing over a bunch of stuff she was angry at him about but hadn't mentioned, letting it build and build to where she was now talking about possibly leaving him.

He was still pondering all of this when the doorbell rang. Startled, he glanced at his watch, unsure of how long he'd been laying there. He rolled off the bed and trudged towards the door, glancing through the peephole. He hesitated when he saw who was on the other side.

"Oh, damn, Serenity," he muttered when he finally swung the door open. "Charmaine isn't here."

"Ace..." Serenity sighed, clearly disappointed. "How is she not here? I called her and asked if I could come by and she insisted it was okay."

"Yeah, she probably did, but we had another argument and she left. I bet she forgot she even told you that."

"Great."

He eyed her. It was clear she'd been crying. "You all right?"

"Not really."

"What's wrong?"

"I know you don't really wanna talk about this with me." She was looking everywhere but at him. "I'm sorry for coming by here so late."

"It's no sweat. You wanna come in for a while? You probably shouldn't be driving around when you're this upset."

"That's all right."

"Serenity, come on," Ace insisted, stepping back and opening the door wider. "I don't know what's going on with you but I figure it must be something pretty major to send you over here at almost ten o'clock at night. We don't have to talk; just come in and chill for a while. I'll just worry about you if you don't."

She turned her red eyes to him before finally nodding, swiping a hand under her eyes. Stepping into the house, she glanced around absently. "Thanks, Ace."

"No prob." He closed the door and stuck his hands in the pockets of his sweats. "You want a drink or something?"

"I've had enough, thank you. I wouldn't mind some water, though."

"I got you." Ace went to the kitchen. When he returned to the living room with a cool bottle of water, Serenity was sitting with her face in her hands on the couch. She looked up when he approached.

"Thanks," she whispered, taking the offered bottle.

"I'll go in the other room. You can stay as long as you need to to get your head together."

Nodding, she unscrewed the cap on the water bottle and took a long gulp. Ace went to the den, simultaneously curious as to what had her so upset and nervous about her being there. He wasn't the best at comforting people, and hoped that some quiet time was all she needed to feel well enough to go back home.

He was watching a music awards show when Serenity wandered into the room.

"Can I join you?" she asked softly. "Sitting in there by myself in the quiet is doing more harm than good."

Ace glanced at her before nodding his head towards the opposite end of the sectional. "Knock yourself out."

She eased down, anxiously rubbing her hands together. A few quiet moments passed. She looked over at him. "No idea when Charmaine will be back, huh?"

Ace took a sip of his soda before pursing his lips. "Nope. No idea. Try calling her, if you want. I doubt she'll answer if I do it."

"Everything okay with you two?"

"Apparently not, if you ask her."

"I know she's had a lot on her mind lately..."

"Yeah, well. Thanks to your man and his let's-tell-all-our-damn-business card game, things haven't been the same between us. Thanks for that."

"Hey, I wasn't all that thrilled about playing that, either, believe me. It opened up a very unwanted can of worms."

"Hmph."

"I'm sorry, Ace." Serenity stood and moved closer to him on the couch. "I hate that what happened at our house caused so much trouble. Taj and I are going through it, you and Charmaine, Lavinia and Ricky-"

"Please, those two didn't need any help. They were a mess way before that."

"True. Unfortunately. I'm actually pretty worried about them. Ricky seems to be at the end of this rope. I don't think alcohol was making him say all those things he said that night. I can only imagine Lavinia was hurt over that, though I know she'd never admit it."

"Yeah, she's got too much pride to be vulnerable like that," Ace agreed, sitting forward to put his soda on the coffee table. "I'm surprised they stayed together this long, really."

"Regardless, I hope they work things out."

"Hmph. That's a long shot."

"What about you and Charmaine? Is that a long shot, too?"

He frowned slightly, eyes still on the television. "I hope not."

"I'm sure you two can get past this, whatever it is."

"You don't have to act like you don't know what it is. Charmaine is one of your girls; I'm sure she's complained to y'all plenty."

"We don't have to talk about this, Ace," Serenity avoided.

"Right, so let's talk about whatever sent you running over here this time of night."

"We don't have to talk about that, either." She slid her fingertips into the nape of her short hair before sliding her hand up and down the back of her neck. "Besides, you can probably guess what my problem is."

Ace sighed. "Serenity-"

"We've never talked about it, you know."

"And we don't need to talk about it now."

Adjusting her off-the-shoulder blouse, Serenity turned towards him fully. "You know I've been tormented ever since then, right? Like, I haven't been able to get it out of my head. And it's driving me crazy."

"I'm sorry to hear that, but-"

"I don't get how *you're* dealing with it so well. Are you just telling yourself it didn't happen?"

His eyes turned to her. "I know it happened. I haven't forgotten."

"Well, what are we gonna do about it? I mean, if Rasheed hadn't saw me on your Facetime-"

"Serenity-"

"No, Ace, we need to discuss this."

"I don't want to discuss it!" Ace barked, shooting up off the couch. She quickly followed suit. "Let's just leave well enough alone."

"It's *not* well enough, though, Ace, that's the point!" Serenity exclaimed. "We're both miserable. Your woman ran off to who knows where and my man is at home cheating on me with some woman in our bed."

"What?!"

"I went home and heard Taj in our room with another woman."

"That doesn't sound like Taj!"

"Well, it *did* sound like Taj; that's why I left. I heard it with my own two ears, Ace."

Shaking his head, Ace frowned thoughtfully. "Nah, Taj isn't like that. What did he say when you confronted him?"

"I didn't. I tried to open the door but it was locked. That's when I called Charmaine; I just wanted to get out of there."

"So you don't even know what the deal really is? Real smart, Serenity. Jumped the gun and got all emotional without knowing all the facts."

Her nostrils flared along with her anger. "I see why Charmaine left. You really can be an insensitive asshole."

His eyebrows lifted slightly. "You said the same thing when we were dating, you know."

"Yeah." Serenity kept her eyes on his. "And we were just teenagers then. Amazing that you haven't changed."

A flash of hurt crossed Ace's eyes before he looked away. "Right. Apparently everybody has a problem with me. You dumped me back in the day. Charmaine is trying to put the brakes on our wedding. Everybody kept telling me to shut up the other night. Maybe I just need to fall back and leave all y'all alone."

"Ace, stop; wait a minute..." Serenity grabbed his arm as he started to turn and walk away from her. "You might have flaws but you're not a terrible person. And for the record, I didn't dump you because I didn't love you anymore. After we lost our baby-"

"Serenity, I said I don't wanna talk about this!" Ace tried to pull away from her.

"We *need* to talk about it!" She jerked him back. "Just like we need to talk about what happened last year! That night changed everything for me, Ace, and it doesn't help that you're just going along like it's nothing. Do you realize things haven't been the same between me and Taj since then? And I don't get how you can look in Charmaine's face everyday knowing you slept with one of her best friends a month after proposing to her!"

"Look, Serenity," he turned to face her. "We don't want each other like that anymore; it was one night of being drunk and stupid. Regardless, it's not like I'm proud of cheating on my lady with you. Even though it didn't mean shit, we were both wrong for taking it there that night and I know that.

There have been a few times that I wanted to tell Charmaine about it and I punked out. But just because I'm not losing my mind over it doesn't mean it doesn't affect me."

"It would help if I could *tell* it affected you," Serenity countered in a softer voice. "Every time I've tried to broach this subject with you since that night, you've avoided it. That's why I've been more nervous around Rasheed than I've been around you; you just don't seem to care."

His eyes fell back to hers. "I care."

"I need you to act like it."

"What is it you want me to do, Serenity? I can't change the past. And I just don't think us rehashing everything that happened will help anything."

"I know what might help me right now..."

"What? If it'll help you feel better and get us off this conversation, I'm down. What would help you right now?"

She eyed his thick lips. "If you kissed me."

He immediately blinked and stepped back, but she tightened her hold on his arm as she quickly closed the distance again. "Serenity..."

"Taj is at our house as we speak fooling around on me. And I've been such a mess for so long that part of me can't even blame him. But right now, right this second, I just want to feel better any way I can. And even though we've both moved on, it doesn't mean I've forgotten how good of a kisser you are...and how those lips feel on me."

Ace couldn't move as she leaned into him, looking up at him with pleading eyes. He felt her large soft breasts press against his chest, and he swallowed, amazed that his body was reacting to her. He thought his attraction to Serenity had been long buried, but with the way his dick was waking up, apparently he was mistaken.

"I *know* it's not right," Serenity continued, sliding her hand down his arm. "And I'm super-emotional right now and probably not thinking straight. But I need this, Ace." She slowly lifted his hand and placed it low on her waist. "Please don't let me feel humiliated for a second time tonight."

He shook his head, taking a small step back. "We can't do this, Serenity."

"Please..."

"It'll only make shit worse."

"It can't get much worse than it is." She quickly closed the distance between them again, pressing against him even more aggressively. Her hand gripped his shirt as they locked eyes. "Ace...I'm begging you."

Everything in Ace's mind and body said he needed to back up and tell Serenity to go home. That nothing good could come from this. But in that moment, he remembered how in love with this woman he used to be, how much she meant to him, and how much he'd missed her after she ended their relationship. It had taken a while for him to ease into a friendship with her after she broke up with him because he'd been so angry about it, but he never once stopped caring about her.

And now all of the forcibly-suppressed memories of the night they shared a year earlier came roaring back. How her soft body felt underneath his. How she responded when he greedily enjoyed licking and sucking and teasing her thick dark nipples; he'd always loved her breasts. She'd been an animal that night, more ravenous than she'd ever been when they were together, and he remembered being pleasantly shocked at how aggressive she was being. She'd devoured him, not being able to keep her hands or her lips from between his legs. His dick twitched at the memory.

All on its own, his hand slid down to her backside and squeezed. Hers eased between them and grazed his hardening erection, making him bite his lip and release a long breath as his eyes slid closed. He felt her other hand slide behind his head and pull him to her, and he offered little resistance. In the next second, his lips were touching hers, and after a few more moments, so was his tongue.

The kisses started out soft and exploratory, as if getting reacquainted with each other. But it didn't take long before the intensity kicked up several notches and they were panting against each other's mouths, their moans overtaking the music coming from the television. Their hands began clawing at each other, each sliding a hand behind the other's waistbands and fondling, both of their heads thrown back in momentary ecstasy.

"This isn't supposed to feel so good," he whispered, hating himself for giving in but unable to stop. "Dammit..."

Serenity stroked him more urgently, fearing his retreat. "It's just one more time. You need this, too, Ace, you know you do. Please don't stop."

"Serenity..."

"Yes, Taj..."

Ace's head snapped up to look at her, his fingers that were teasing her clit slowing.

Realizing her words, Serenity frantically looked at him as she grabbed his hand, moving against it and urging him to continue. "Don't stop...we both know what this is. Just keep going, please, Ace..."

"Serenity..." he breathed, licking his lips. "Maybe we should...ooh, *fuck*!"

She had yanked his pants down, dropped to her knees and taken him into her mouth with way more enthusiasm than she'd been able to muster for Taj a few nights earlier. Ace's hand grabbed the back of her head as he pumped into her mouth, unable to deny how good it felt as his waning resistance finally evaporated. In the back of his mind, he *knew* they should stop, but he was getting into 'too far gone' territory. With everything going on between him and Charmaine lately, it felt good to turn his mind off and just enjoy some pleasure. It felt good to be wanted. Charmaine's legs had been clamped since couple's night, and he'd been extremely sexually frustrated. And as wrong as he knew this was, he couldn't make himself forget that right then.

Serenity pushed him onto the couch before quickly shimmying out of her cotton panties. She lifted her long skirt and climbed onto him, their kiss quickly resuming. The sound of ripping fabric broke through as Ace yanked her shirt and bra to the side and took her thick nipple into his mouth, grunting at how it felt just as good as he remembered. Serenity cried out in pleasure, holding his head close as she began to grind on him.

"Shit, Serenity," Ace whispered, his hand underneath her skirt squeezing her plump ass. His hips matched her now-hectic rhythm. His head fell back momentarily as he frowned and released an anguished groan at how amazing she felt on him. "You're *so* wet..."

She took his face in her hands and kissed him hard, their tongues tangling in an erotic battle. He returned her kiss with equal need, his hand still gripping her left breast as if he couldn't let it go.

"I wanna feel you inside of me," she panted against his lips between their erotically-sloppy kisses. "Right now."

Officially too far gone, Ace quickly nodded. "You wanna fuck?"

"Yes. Oh god, yes; *please* fuck me, Ace."

"I don't have any condoms."

"Just for a minute. I just need to feel you, Ace, please. Just let me know when you're about to-*ahhhhhh*..."

He had lifted her high enough so he could slide inside of her, and they both hissed at the familiar pleasure. Tears immediately came to Serenity's eyes at how amazingly delicious it felt; why couldn't she be this uninhibited with Taj? He was who she loved.

But then she remembered what Taj was doing right then, and her hips began moving more frantically. Pretty soon she was bouncing hard on Ace's dick as he held her hips and met her stroke for stroke, looking at her face that was displaying a remorseful pleasure.

"This what you wanted?" he asked her, slapping her ass underneath her skirt. "Is our minute up?"

"No..." She frantically shook her head. "No, I don't wanna stop yet."

"I didn't think so."

He leaned forward and started teasing her nipples again, gripping her ass with both hands as their hard sexing switched to a smooth grind. They urged each other on, taunting and pleading, each of them forgetting about any and everything else. Ace tossed her onto her back and quickly slid back inside of her, pounding into her as his hands gripped the back of the couch.

"Harder," Serenity pleaded. "Fuck me harder, Ace."

He didn't speak; he just obeyed. Her jaw fell slack as she readily took everything he was giving her, everything she asked for, trying to resist screaming like she wanted to as her thick legs opened as wide as they could go and her hands gripped his backside, pulling him into her. Their talking had ceased as they each just reveled in their selfish momentary pleasure, forgetting where they were or who they were supposed to belong to.

Just like that night a year before, Serenity couldn't get enough. She hurried onto her knees as she looked back at him pleadingly, and Ace wasted no time obliging her silent request. His hands gripped her waist, his brow furrowed as he watched himself go in and out of her, their skin slapping so hard it drowned out the television. Serenity's voice wavered with each hard thrust, loving the pleasurable punishment.

"I'm 'bout to come," Ace grunted. "Fuck, I'm gonna bust-"

"No, not like this...lemme ride you again," Serenity urged, her hand pushing at his thigh. In the next few seconds she was back on his lap, wildly bucking on him as his head fell against the back of the couch. Their eyes were closed as they each focused on reaching their own high. His thrusts got more erratic and Serenity knew he was getting close, and she grabbed his hands and placed them on her aching breasts underneath her askew bra as her own orgasm started to build, tears of guilty pleasure streaming down her face.

"I'm so close," she whimpered, biting her lip, her hands that were covering his on her breasts tensing as her hips moved faster. "Oh god, yes!"

"You gonna come on this dick?"

"Yes! Yes!"

"I'm gonna nut...I need to pull out-"

"No, please! I'm on the pill, I swear! It feels too good, please-"

Suddenly they heard the front door slam and reality washed back over them like a cold splash.

"Ace?"

Freezing instantly at the sound of Charmaine's voice, Serenity and Ace looked at each other in wide-eyed panic before she scrambled off his lap, righting her bra and shirt and fluffing out her short hair. Ace frantically yanked his pants and boxers up, glancing at Serenity, who he could tell was on the verge of panicking.

"Hey, get it together," he hissed. Standing, he held his untied sweats up with his hand and shot her a warning glance. "*This didn't happen*. You hear me?"

Before Serenity could respond, he scrambled down the hallway towards the guest bathroom. Serenity noticed her panties on the floor and gasped, snatching them up right before Charmaine appeared in the doorway to the den, looking remorseful. Serenity fought to keep her face even, despite wiping her sex-high tears.

"Girl, I am *so* sorry," Charmaine exclaimed, quickly coming towards her. She dropped down next to Serenity on the couch and wrapped her arms around her, squeezing her in a hug as Serenity tried to discreetly tuck her panties into her skirt pocket. "I got so mad at Ace earlier and ran out of here, totally forgetting I'd said you could come over. Are you okay? Aww, you've been crying..."

Serenity averted her eyes, knowing her tears weren't for the reason Charmaine thought they were. That might've been the case when she arrived at their house but now... "It's okay. I-I totally understand. I just needed to get away from the house."

"What happened? Taj didn't put you out, did he?"

Serenity was too busy worrying that Charmaine would smell the sex in the air that she didn't hear the question at first. "Huh? I'm sorry, wh-what did you say?"

"Wow, girl, you must be really going through it. I asked if Taj had put you out and that's why you needed to come over."

"Oh...um, no, it's not that. I'm sorry; at this point, I'm just too tired to talk about it." Her face was still averted; she couldn't look at her friend that she'd just stabbed in the back. Again.

"I'm so sorry for not being here when you needed me." Charmaine's hand rubbed her back as she glanced around. "Where's Ace?"

Immediately tensing, Serenity cleared her throat. "Umm, I'm not sure...I guess he went to the back or something. He just told me I could sit and get my head together."

"And, what, he made himself scarce instead of keeping you company? I wouldn't be surprised. Emotional stuff isn't his strong suit. He's liable to do or say something stupid."

We both did that, Serenity immediately thought. She glanced down, and that's when she noticed the small tear in her shirt. She quickly clutched it in her hand, still able to feel Ace's tongue on her skin.

"He, um, he was fine. He actually..." She sniffled. "He was pretty eager to help. Eventually."

"Really? Well, I'm glad that he didn't make things any worse." Charmaine paused, frowning slightly. "What's that smell? You smell that?"

Her face flaming, Serenity wished she could vanish into thin air. She knew Charmaine would be able to tell something had gone down. "Oh...well, you know how Taj and I have been having our issues in the bedroom. I might've taken the opportunity while I was alone to..." She made herself glance at Charmaine pointedly. "You know."

Her face brightening in realization, Charmaine nodded. "Ohh. Hey, I totally get it. Sometimes you've just gotta do what you've gotta do, girl, and relieve that tension. Is that why you're looking so embarrassed?"

"Pretty much. And, um...what's worse, I think Ace probably heard me. That's why he's made himself so scarce."

"Girl, you don't have to be embarrassed about that. There's nothing wrong with masturbating to take the edge off." She leaned in closer. "Between you and me, things haven't exactly been great between me and Ace when it comes to that lately, either. He's been wanting it but I keep shutting him down; I guess as a way to punish him or something. And I'm not proud of this, but, well...you know Tango, from the bakery?"

Serenity's eyes snapped to her. "Yeah..."

"*Well-*"

"Babe, I didn't hear you come in," Ace interrupted, entering the room fully dressed and clear-faced as if he didn't have a care in the world. He picked up his soda from the coffee table and drained the rest of it.

Charmaine cut her eyes at him, apparently not happy about her confession being cut short. "Yeah, I came back when I remembered I told Serenity she could come by. What were you doing?"

"Had to take a call," he replied easily.

"Oh. Well, thanks for letting Serenity come in and get her head together. Though I don't know why you didn't call me and let me know she was here."

"For what? You're the one that ran out of here with an attitude. Figured you wouldn't have answered my call, anyway."

Charmaine pursed her lips, knowing she probably wouldn't have.

Needing to get out of there, Serenity shot up off the couch, startling Charmaine. "I'm gonna go, you guys. It's late and I should get home."

"You sure? You can spend the night if you need to," Charmaine offered.

"Oh no," Serenity quickly protested. Her hand gripped her pocket, making sure her discarded panties were securely inside. "That's not necessary. I just want to get in my own bed and push everything that happened tonight out of my mind." She shot a brief glance at Ace before reaching down to grab her purse.

"I understand. I'm gonna be doing the same thing." Charmaine shot her own glance at Ace, who just glared at her.

"Thanks for the reprieve." Serenity forced a smile down at Charmaine even though she was mostly speaking to Ace. "I needed it."

"No problem, girl. Call me tomorrow."

"I will." Serenity headed for the door, a warm wave washing over her as she passed by Ace. "Good night."

"Good night, Serenity." He glanced her way before sinking onto the couch and grabbing the remote.

As soon as she was back in her car, Serenity noticed her hands were shaking. Realization of what she had just done began to overtake her like an unwanted pursuer.

"Damn it!" she screamed as she hit the steering wheel with both palms. "Damn it, *damn it*, DAMN IT!!"

Chapter 11

The friends were meeting up, the men separate from the women, to drink and vent about their current situations. Ricky, Ace, Taj, and Rasheed were gathered at Fourth and Long, a local sports bar, though some were less enthusiastic about being there than others.

It'd been less than a week since his latest indiscretion with Serenity, and Ace was having a hard time looking at his boy, Taj. It had been eating at him, the fact that he lost his head like that. It was one thing to get with Serenity in some random hotel out of town, but quite another to sex her on the same couch his fiancée sat on everyday in their den. It was only because Charmaine was still miffed at him that he was even able to stay in the same house with her after that. It was one time he was glad they weren't really speaking.

"I see we're all going through it," Rasheed surmised, glancing around the back table they were all seated at. A major college football game was playing on the television above their table but they were barely paying it any attention. "All y'all look like shit."

They glared at him. "You're not exactly about to be on anybody's billboard any time soon, either," Ricky retorted. "When's the last time you did something to that scruffy-ass beard?"

"Don't be worrying about my beard. Iman likes it."

"Uh-huh. Still punking out about telling her you want her to be your woman?"

Rasheed frowned, but sighed and plunked back in his seat. "I'm just not trying to make a fool out of myself."

"Why do you think you'd be doing that? Iman might be feeling you like you're feeling her," Taj replied.

"But she might *not* be. Not to mention, she's been hella distant lately; the last few times I called her to hook up, she always had an excuse why she can't. She didn't used to do that. You think she's met somebody else? Have any of y'all's ladies said anything?"

"Hmph," Ace scoffed, taking an angry gulp of his beer. "You know Charmaine doesn't have many words for me lately."

"And Serenity has been too busy crying and sleeping on the couch to gossip about y'all," Taj muttered. Ace shifted in his seat.

"I'm still at the hotel," Ricky announced. "Ever since I heard Lavinia talking shit to her mother about me, I haven't been to the house. Other than to get some work stuff when I knew they weren't there."

They all looked at him. "Damn, man, I thought you'd have gone back by now," Taj admitted. "How long are you gonna keep this up? Has she called?"

"Hell yeah, she's been blowing my phone up. I don't have anything to say to her."

"How are you gonna work things out if you don't talk to her, though?" Rasheed asked.

"I'm not sure I *want* to work it out," Ricky mumbled, pushing his glass back and forth between his hands. His locs hung in his face, out of their usual ponytail, and he looked like he hadn't been sleeping much. His eyes looked weary. "I think it might be time to just accept that Lavinia and I don't work and let it go."

The men reared in shock. They of course knew that their friend hadn't exactly been happy with Lavinia, but they hadn't expected him to seriously consider leaving her.

"Ricky, man..." Taj ventured, sitting forward in his seat and looking at his friend intently, "Are you sure that's what you wanna do? You and Lavinia have been married for over eleven years. Why not try to make it work?'

"'Cause it can't just be *me* wanting to make it work," Ricky retorted. He pushed his glass away and sat back in his chair. "I'd actually be open to going to marriage counseling. Hell, I'm already seeing a therapist so I can even tolerate being around her as it is. But Lavinia refuses to admit her part in all this. Let her tell it, she's not doing anything wrong. Therapy is pointless if we're not both willing to make changes."

"Wow. I just hate to see y'all split up like this over something that could be fixable."

"What about *you*?" Ricky countered. "You and Serenity aren't exactly living in bliss. You won't even propose to her. And you said yourself she's been sleeping on the couch. What about that?"

Taj's frown was immediate. "I'm not gonna lie; our relationship is kind of a mess. I love Serenity, but I'm not sure how much longer we can go on like this."

"That's surprising. I thought when Ace introduced you two that you were damn near perfect for each other."

Ace grunted before he could stop himself, and the other men looked at him. He tried to play it off with a shrug. "What do I know? Clearly, I can't even keep my own woman happy."

"Y'all are fighting again?" Rasheed asked.

"Man, she gave me a damn ultimatum. Said she didn't think we were ready to get married...no, that I'm 'too thoughtless to be anybody's husband'. Straight up said we're done if I don't agree to go to counseling or do something else to fix things."

"Okay, so go to counseling," Taj instructed with a shrug. "Hell, I *wish* that's all Serenity and I needed to do. She's been so different over this past year, like she's scared to touch me or something. But of course, she's glad to *receive* all the orgasms. Our sex life has been frustratingly one-sided, if you can even call it a sex life. It's all been just oral and glorified petting, really. I got more action back in college."

"And you don't know what might have caused that? There has to be a reason she switched up out of the blue," Ricky commented.

Ace looked up from his glass to see Rasheed peering at him pointedly. He knew Rasheed wanted him to go ahead and admit his transgression with Serenity, but it was way easier said than done. He looked away, signaling to the waitress for another beer.

"She gave me some explanation saying that..." Taj's voice trailed off before shaking his head. "Doesn't matter. It didn't change anything. What she told me was so out of left field and even after she supposedly unburdened herself, she was still so skittish in the bedroom that she busted out crying when she was giving me head. Has barely slept in the same bed with me since. Clearly, there's still something going on."

Ace winced, remembering Serenity on her knees in front of him in his den just days earlier. She certainly hadn't been skittish then. She was the aggressive, wonton, super-sensual vixen she'd been when they were together back in the day. It didn't make him feel good to know he had gotten what his boy was supposed to be getting. Taj didn't even know that he and Serenity used to be in a relationship, because Ace hadn't thought it mattered. It was so long ago, after all. But now he was wondering if he'd been wrong about that.

Rasheed was trying to send a silent signal to Ace to just come out with it. For Ace's benefit but also his own. He was tired of keeping Ace and Serenity's secret, and felt as guilty as the two of them for Taj being in the dark. It was clear that Serenity's guilt was affecting her performance in the bedroom with Taj. Rasheed wished he'd never Facetimed Ace that night; then he wouldn't have seen a naked Serenity coming out of the bathroom in the background.

"I hope y'all can work it out, man," Ricky commented. "Believe me, I know how bad communication and being on two different pages can kill a relationship."

The four friends nursed their beers, with Taj keeping his eyes on his glass, Ricky glancing at yet another incoming message from Lavinia on his phone, Ace feigning interest in the football game, and Rasheed glaring at Ace.

Meanwhile, the ladies were gathered at Iman's apartment, equally as glum. It took a lot of bugging on Iman's part to even get Serenity to agree to show up; the guilt over what she'd done with Ace had her scared to death to be around Charmaine.

"Lavinia, will you put your phone down?" Charmaine requested. "You've been texting Ricky since you got here. Give him time to respond."

"Clearly he *won't* respond," Lavinia retorted, furiously typing out another pleading text to her husband. "He's been ignoring me since he moved out without a word."

"I still can't believe he hasn't come home yet," Iman commented. "I mean, I know he was pretty ticked at you but for him to actually go stay at a hotel?"

"I've wanted to go look for him but I kept thinking he would come back on his own," Lavinia admitted, eyes on her phone that she was holding in her lap in both hands. "I knew he wasn't happy about Mama coming to stay with us but I didn't think it was this big a deal."

"I'm sure it's about more than that. That *can't* be the only thing that sent him packing."

"Truth be told, y'all, I thought about going to a hotel a few times, myself," Charmaine admitted. "I just haven't wanted to be around Ace lately. Talk about stubborn...I told him we needed to do something to fix things or we'd have to break up."

They all looked at her, alarmed. "You really gave him an ultimatum?" Iman asked.

"At the time I didn't even really mean it; it just came out," Charmaine admitted. "I mean, I love Ace, y'all; I really do. But is he *really* ready to be a husband? He just says the first thing that comes to his mind, he makes decisions without consulting or considering me, he acts first and thinks second. I can't deal with years and years of that."

"At least Ace is willing to stay and work things out with you, though," Lavinia muttered. She finally plunked her phone next to her on the couch and ran a hand through her long professionally-done weave. Her turtleneck and jeans were a far cry from the revealing clothing she usually wore. "Ricky acts like he can't even stand the sight of me."

"Well, it's not like I'm Taj's favorite person lately, either," Serenity finally spoke up. She was curled up in the corner of the couch, playing with the edge of the pillow hugged to her chest. "But I know it's my own fault."

"Girl, what *is* going on with you two?" Charmaine asked, leaning forward. "Y'all were so happy at first. I thought you were the perfect couple."

Serenity kept her eyes on the floor, unable to look at her friend. The replay of herself pleading with Ace to kiss her, touch her, fuck her, blasted through her head for the thousandth time since it happened, causing her to wince slightly at the memory. She'd even been so far gone she hadn't cared about protection and was going to let him come inside of her, and that realization was so humiliating it made her skin burn. "Yeah, that's what we wanted people to think. Or at least, I did. I didn't even want to acknowledge the issues we had...I guess I thought not admitting to them wouldn't give them any power and they wouldn't truly exist."

"Keeping stuff buried like that can only do more harm than good, girl," Iman spoke up. "It just keeps eating at you until it drives you nuts. Whatever issues you and Taj have, it's best to just get everything out in the open and deal with it so you can move on."

Knowing she didn't have the nerve to follow that completely sensible advice, Serenity just gave a slight nod and kept pinching the corner of the pillow. "Yeah."

"And what about *you*, Iman?" Charmaine said, turning the tables. "When are you going to stop wasting time and finally tell Rasheed how you really feel about him?"

Clamming up, Iman shrunk in her seat, suddenly becoming fascinated with the ends of her braids. "I don't know. Maybe it was a mistake for me and Rasheed to start fooling around together."

"Why do you say that?" Lavinia asked.

"Because I wasn't expecting to catch feelings for him like I did. This was supposed to be something light and breezy but I almost lost it when I saw some other woman flirting with him."

"Okay, so things changed. That's not a bad thing. Just tell him."

"It's not the easiest thing in the world to admit, Lavinia."

"Okay, so? Since when have you been so shy? He might want the same thing you want."

"I can't tell that."

"Please, men don't always say what's on their minds," Charmaine scoffed. "Well, Ace does. But a lot don't. You can't drop hints; you just have to come out with it. I see how he looks at you; I'm willing to bet just about anything that he'd be more than happy to be your man."

"Y'all, I've been here before...told someone how I felt about them, all but sure he was feeling me like I was feeling him, and ended up humiliated when he shut me down, even though he was nice about it. I can't deal with that again."

"That was then, Iman. Whoever that was isn't Rasheed. You can't assume the same thing will happen with him."

"I'm sorry, Iman, but it's a little hard for me to have a lot of sympathy for you when my husband is halfway out the door,"

Lavinia grumbled. "Not to mention what's going on with Serenity and Taj, and Charmaine and Ace. We're dealing with some *real* shit. You and Rasheed being too scared to admit you're feeling each other is some teenage stuff."

"Excuse me?" Iman frowned. "Just because it's not on the same level as what y'all are dealing with doesn't mean it doesn't matter."

"It's easily fixable, though. You're just being a punk about it."

"Be quiet, Lavinia. Maybe it's your smart-ass mouth that sent your husband packing. You ever think of that?"

"Come on," Charmaine called out before Lavinia could respond, holding her arms out and looking back and forth between them. "Let's not start snapping on each other."

"Tell your girl to watch her damn mouth, then," Iman warned, scowling at Lavinia.

"Try to remember she's going through it with Ricky, Iman."

"Yeah, so? You and Serenity are having issues, too, but neither of y'all are showing your ass and being dismissive. 'Cause please believe, I can get all the way real and say what I *really* think about her *and* her husband."

"Well, speak your mind, then!" Lavinia exclaimed, tossing her phone down next to her and scooting forward in her seat. "Come on with it!"

"Guys, no! Stop!" Charmaine pleaded as Iman was ready to launch into her diatribe. "Us turning on each other isn't gonna help anything. We're supposed to be friends, remember?"

"And friends keep it real with each other," Lavinia spoke up. "All I'm saying is, Iman, that you're making it harder than it needs to be. You and Rasheed keep dancing around the subject when all one of you has to do is just-"

"Maybe I'm afraid I'll lose him! Did you ever consider that??" Iman practically yelled. "Just because I'm self-assured and confident about other things doesn't mean it's that easy for me to put myself out there like that with the man I'm falling for! If he rejected me, it would change *everything*!"

The ladies went silent, shocked. None of them knew how deep Iman's feelings for Rasheed ran, because she always gave the impression that they *weren't* that deep; she'd insist that she enjoyed hanging with him and sexing him, but wouldn't be affected if it ever stopped. But apparently she'd been just as dishonest with herself as she'd been with them.

"Wow, Iman," Serenity whispered.

"Girl..." Lavinia hedged, looking uncharacteristically remorseful. "I didn't know it was like that. You actually love Rasheed?"

Iman hunched a shoulder. "I think I do. That's what makes this so difficult; I was feeling that other guy but it was *nothing* like what I feel for Rasheed. But I've never really been in love before so...how do I even know that? How can I be sure?"

"When you know, you know," Charmaine insisted, going to put her arm around Iman. "Believe me, when it's real, there won't be a doubt in your mind."

"That's true," Lavinia cosigned. "I can certainly remember when I knew I loved Ricky. We hadn't even been dating that long when I knew he had me. Went right over to his place in the middle of the night to tell him."

"And how did he respond?" Iman asked her.

"I definitely threw him for a loop. He wasn't quite where I was but insisted that he felt he could be. Actually said he was glad I let him know; that way he knew we were both on the same page and not just dating for the hell of it."

Iman pondered this for a moment before looking over at Serenity. "What about you? When did you know you'd fallen for Taj?"

Serenity's reminiscent smile was automatic. "Like with Lavinia, it didn't take me long. I knew after our first date that he was it for me. He totally had my heart after a month. Though I admit it took me a while to admit that to him because I was afraid I'd scare him off."

"So when did you tell him?"

"I waited for him to admit it to me first. Every time I started to bring up my feelings to him, I lost my nerve."

"So you get where I'm coming from, then!"

"Yeah, I totally get it, Iman, but I don't exactly think you should follow my example. Being afraid to have uncomfortable conversations isn't a good thing at all; you don't know what you might miss out on or lose because of it." Serenity shifted in her seat, her smile fading. "It might've worked out in my case but that's not how it goes every time."

Her face took on a pained expression before she hastily moved the pillow in her lap to the side and stood, hurrying out of the room. Her friends all looked after her before turning confused and concerned expressions towards each other.

"She must *really* be going through it with Taj," Lavinia commented.

Charmaine nodded. "Yeah, she hasn't been herself all night. Really, she's been distant for a while now. She certainly seemed strange when she was at my house the other night."

"There has to be more to it that we don't know," Iman added, casting a worried glance in the direction Serenity had scurried off to. "I know she said they were having trouble in the bedroom but that can't be all it is; not with how emotional she's been."

"You're right. I wonder why she won't tell us what it is, though. She should know she can confide in us without judgment." Charmaine looked at Iman and Lavinia. "And she hasn't said anything to either of you?"

They both shook their heads. "Nope," Iman replied. "She clams up whenever I've tried to ask her about it. Really though, I think Rasheed knows whatever it is."

The women looked at her. "How would Rasheed know?" Lavinia asked.

"Beats me. But I had confronted him after couple's night because I thought maybe the two of them had fooled around or something, because she seemed awfully nervous around him. But he swore it wasn't anything like that; said there was something she was keeping from Taj but it wasn't his place to tell me what it is."

"Wow..." Charmaine marveled. "And apparently, she still hasn't come clean about whatever it is, if she's still this anguished."

"Must be something huge," Lavinia added. "At couple's night, she said it involved someone in the room. I wonder..."

Just then, Serenity re-entered the room, but she didn't reclaim her seat on the couch. She just stood in the middle of the living room, looking at the ground with her hand on her chest.

"I *have* to get this out," she began, her voice cracking. It was clear she'd been crying. "I can't keep going like this."

"Girl, what's the matter?" Lavinia asked her. "You look like you're in pain."

"Serenity, you know you can tell us anything," Iman assured. She stood and went over to comfort Serenity, who stepped away from her touch.

"Please don't," she whimpered. "I don't deserve any comforting. You'll all probably hate me after you hear what I have to say."

"Serenity, what are you talking about? We could *never* hate you, girl," Charmaine insisted. "If you've messed up, we'll be here for you, you know that."

Immediately shaking her head, Serenity retorted, "Not this time."

They all looked at her strangely, their curiosity going through the roof. It was in that moment that they all knew that whatever was troubling Serenity would be something that would change things.

"What could *you*, Serenity Cook, have done that's so bad?" Lavinia asked her. "You've been like a grown girl scout ever since I've known you. It's not in you to do anything *that* terrible."

Serenity realized her friends really didn't know her as well as they thought they did, and that was her fault. She'd always been so concerned about coming across as someone that had it all together and who wouldn't so much as raise her voice in anger that she hadn't kept it real with them over the years. All that time she'd spent worrying about her and Taj *looking* like they had the perfect relationship that she didn't do what was necessary for them to actually have it, or as close to it as they could get.

She'd brought all this mess on herself. And now it was time to start being honest about it. Of course Taj should've been the one who got the first confession, but he wasn't there. And she couldn't keep looking at Charmaine and take her being so nice and supportive, knowing what she'd done.

"I so wish that were true, Lavinia," Serenity finally sighed. "You have no idea."

Her friends waited patiently as she ran both hands through her hair and took several deep breaths. She was scared to death but knew she had to come clean; the guilt had been making her physically sick.

"There's a reason I haven't been able to...*be* with Taj the way I used to," she began, her eyes still on the ground and both hands clasping the back of her neck. "A little over a year ago, I...I cheated on him."

The ladies gasped.

"And the guilt has been eating at me ever since," Serenity continued. "But the fact that I cheated isn't even the worst part; it's who it was with."

"Who was it?" Lavinia immediately demanded. "Wait, was it Ricky??"

"Lavinia, hush!" Iman frowned. "Let her get it out."

Shifting her weight back and forth, Serenity slowly turned her eyes to Charmaine. It didn't take long for realization to hit.

"You mean...?" Charmaine's eyes widened as she grabbed the arm of the couch.

"Ace and I dated a long time ago," Serenity forged ahead, desperation in her voice. "We were teenagers, but we were together for over two years. We got pregnant when we were nineteen and ended up losing the baby; after that, he and I started butting heads a lot more and I ended it."

Their jaws on the ground, Charmaine, Lavinia, and Iman stared at Serenity as if they expected her to start laughing and tell them it was just a joke. But that didn't happen.

"We were out of touch for years and both moved on," Serenity continued. "By the time we reconnected, he was seeing you, Charmaine. Then he introduced me to Taj..."

"So why haven't you said anything about this before now?" Charmaine demanded.

"We figured there was no need in saying anything, since it was so long ago," Serenity replied. "What we had was over with."

"So that's why you've been acting like you have? Because you and Ace used to date and you never told anybody?" Lavina verified. "Does Taj know?"

"No. It's just one of many things I haven't been honest with Taj about. I don't even deserve for him to propose to me."

"So what else aren't you telling us?" Charmaine asked, sensing there was more to this confession. Her patience had fizzled, knowing it involved her fiancé. "What else haven't you been honest about?"

Her hands shaking, Serenity made herself look at her friend. They shared a look, Charmaine's nostrils slightly flared and her chest heaving in anticipation. Iman, having already put two-and-two together, moved to stand between the ladies.

"It was Ace," Serenity finally confirmed. Tears streamed down her face. "About a year ago, I slept with Ace, Charmaine, and I can't even *tell* you how sorry I am..."

Even though she sensed that's where Serenity was going with it, Charmaine still reeled at hearing it declared. Her mouth fell open but nothing came out, and she began rocking back and forth in her seat. Lavinia reached over and grabbed her arm, because it looked like she was going to explode at any second.

Knowing there was more she needed to admit to, Serenity made herself speak again. "Unfortunately, that's not all."

Iman looked at her, shaking her head. "Maybe you should let her process what you've already told her first before you add anything else."

"No, Iman, I have to get it all out now or I won't be able to keep living with myself. I've been sick over this for too long." Serenity tried to still her trembling hands by clutching her shirt. "It wasn't a one-time thing."

"What??" Lavinia shouted, as Charmaine's red eyes snapped up in alarm. Iman groaned.

"The other night, when I asked to come over and Ace and I were alone, we got to talking about the past and everything, and I-I admit I came on to him," Serenity admitted tearfully. "I was upset about Taj cheating on me in our bed and I just wanted to feel better-"

"What, what?? Taj had some other woman in your house??" Iman exclaimed.

"That's why I had called Charmaine and asked if I could come over; I heard them through the bedroom door," Serenity answered. "I *know* it's no excuse but Ace was there and I got to remembering things from that night last year, and between the couple of drinks I'd had and being mad at Taj, I just lost my head. Charmaine, please-"

"So you made a move on my fiancé??" Charmaine screamed, shooting up from the couch. Lavinia hurriedly stood to hold her back. "You fooled around with my man in my house??"

"I'm sorry!"

"Then you lied to my face, talking about you were just masturbating while he was in the other room?? I *knew* that didn't sound right when you said it but I never thought you would've stabbed me in the back like that!"

"It didn't mean anything, Charmaine, I swear!" Serenity pleaded from behind Iman, who was shielding her from a furious Charmaine. "And I know it didn't mean anything to Ace, either! He still wants you and I just want Taj! I...we just got caught up in the moment but I felt sick as soon as it was over. I knew I'd made yet another mistake."

"Mistake?? Bitch, *you fucked my man in my house!*" Charmaine charged towards Serenity before Lavinia could stop her, and Serenity screamed. Lavinia and Iman tried to hold Charmaine off, but she wasn't going to be easily deterred. The rage in her eyes was clear as she clawed at Serenity's face, her nails scraping the side of her neck.

"Charmaine!" Lavinia yelled, finally managing to pull her back by the waist. She outweighed Charmaine by a significant amount but the adrenaline coursing through Charmaine's body had her stronger than a raging bull. "Charmaine, stop!"

"Get off me, Lavinia!"

"No! Even if she does need her ass beat for that trifling shit she did, that's not gonna change anything!"

"It'll make me feel better!"

"Charmaine-"

"Serenity, just shut up right now, okay?" Iman ordered, turning a warning look at her while still keeping an eye on Charmaine. "Don't make it worse!"

"I cannot *believe* this!" Charmaine exclaimed, still trying to break free of Lavinia's grasp. "I thought we were friends, Serenity! How could you do this shit? How could *Ace* do this??"

"Ace resisted me at first but I kept pressing him," Serenity insisted, her makeup now streaked from all the tears. Her hand was pressed over the stinging spot where Charmaine had clawed her. "He wasn't even in the same room as me but I went to him. I'm the one that insisted on talking about the past and igniting all those emotions. This is all on me; I started it and kept pushing for more. Hate me but don't hate Ace!"

Charmaine charged at Serenity again, trying to push past Iman. "Oh I think I have enough for the *both* of you!"

"Charmaine!" Lavinia finally managed to hurl Charmaine back onto the couch, and Charmaine immediately burst into tears, the weight of everything finally hitting her. She fell onto her side, face covering her hands as the sobs wracked her body. Lavinia quickly went over and wrapped her arms around her friend, holding her head to her chest and wincing in compassion at her friend's loud wails.

Serenity looked at her devastated friend and knew things would never be the same between them. She wished there was something she could do or say to make things better, but she knew there wasn't. She'd committed the ultimate betrayal and knew it would take an act of God to even get Charmaine to forgive her, let alone them getting any semblance of their friendship back.

Iman looked at her, the weight of the situation getting to her, too. The emotions and heavy situation had brought tears to her own eyes, also knowing their friendship circle was probably permanently damaged.

"Maybe you should go," she told Serenity in a low voice.

Serenity didn't want to leave, but figured nothing good could come from her staying there. Nodding sadly, she swiped at her flowing tears before easing over to grab her purse from near the couch. Charmaine and Lavinia shot her evil glares, the tears still streaming down Charmaine's face.

"I am so sorry," Serenity couldn't resist saying to her. "I love you so much, Charmaine, and I understand if you can't forgive me for this. But I am truly, sincerely sorry."

With that, Serenity turned and walked out, wondering if she'd just lost her friends for good.

Chapter 12

While the women were facing off, Rasheed was cornering Ace.

"I'm tired of keeping this secret, man," Rasheed hissed at him. "You need to tell Taj what went down with you and Serenity and just get it over with."

"You say that like it's easy," Ace scoffed. "Like it's nothing to tell my boy that I cheated on my woman with his."

"I know it's not easy. But maybe you should've thought about that before you slept with her." At Ace's glare, Rasheed pressed on. "Hey, don't even try getting mad at *me*. I'm not the one you need to be worried about. Did you really think you'd be able to hide things forever?"

"No, man," Ace grumbled, running his hands down his face. "Just because I don't act like it doesn't mean it doesn't bother me. Charmaine's a good woman and I love her; I *hate* knowing I did this to her."

"Well then tell her about it."

"That'll be just like pushing her out the door, 'Sheed. She's practically one foot out, as it is."

"Again, you should've considered that before. I'm not trying to rub it in but you know you'd want to know if she stepped out on you, especially since you're planning on getting married." He clamped a hand on Ace's shoulder. "If you really love her, man, you've gotta keep it a hundred with her. Man up."

Ace knew he was right but that didn't ease his fear. He was sure Charmaine would leave him as soon as she found

140

out about him and Serenity. But Rasheed was right about him wanting to know the truth if the roles were reversed.

"Yeah," he eventually grunted.

"And you've gotta tell Taj, too," Rasheed continued. "Y'all are boys."

"Why can't Serenity be the one to tell him?"

"Her telling him and you telling him are two different things. You know he's gonna feel some kind of way if he finds out about this and realizes you spent all this time in his face without saying anything."

Ace saw Rasheed's point. He and Taj were boys and he'd definitely broken the code. Ace didn't even know if or when Serenity was planning to come clean with Taj, but even if she did, that still didn't absolve him from having his own conversation with Taj. He had to stop being a punk and own up to his actions.

And Rasheed didn't even know about his and Serenity's latest mistake. As amazing as it had felt in the moment, Ace was kicking himself as soon as he'd went off to another room when Charmaine came home that night. It had taken *every* ounce of control to act cool in front of her.

But maybe since Taj had apparently cheated himself, he wouldn't blow up *too* much.

When they got back to the table, Ace told himself to just come out with it. But Ricky's admission made both him and Rasheed temporarily forget about anything to do with Serenity.

"What did you just say?" Rasheed marveled.

"I said I'm gonna divorce Lavinia," Ricky confirmed. "I just made the decision."

"Just now?"

"Yep."

"What made you come to that?" Taj asked.

"Because these last few days away from Lavinia have brought me more peace than I've had in years. I don't even miss her. And that has to mean something."

"Yeah, it means you two have some serious problems and need to work on your relationship."

"Taj, man, that's what I've been telling y'all...I've tried all that. I'm not saying I'm perfect by any means but Lavinia is the one that won't cooperate. She actually called me weak for going to a therapist on my own; you think a woman like that is going to ever be open to changing anything?"

"She actually said that? That you were weak?" Ace asked.

"Yeah, she did. Why would I want to be with a woman like that? Nah, this marriage is *done*."

The men sat in surprised silence. They never thought Ricky would get to the point where he declared wanting to leave Lavinia for good. It was one thing to muse about it but another to make the decision to actually do it.

"Ricky..." Taj hedged. "Are you *sure* about this, man?"

"Yeah." Ricky drained his glass and clunked it back onto the table, nodding vigorously as if to reassure himself. "Yeah, I'm sure. Not all marriages last forever. And I can't stay with a woman that doesn't respect me."

Just then, his phone chimed with another text from Lavinia. He sucked his teeth, making no move to read it.

"She's been blowing you up all night, man," Rasheed pointed out, nodding towards the phone. "Maybe she's ready to work on things."

"Yeah, maybe you being gone made her realize what she might be losing," Taj added. "Look, we've all been around Lavinia enough to know she's not the easiest to deal with. And I know we've been on you in the past about standing up to her more. But-"

"And that's what I'm doing," Ricky cut in. "I'm tired, y'all. Tired of being married to a woman who's selfish and stubborn and has no respect for me as a man or as her husband. And if I hear 'happy wife, happy life' one more time I'm gonna lose my damn mind."

"Yeah, I always thought that was some bullshit, too," Ace agreed. "Something women made up to get their way all the time. Thankfully Charmaine never said that mess."

The mention of Charmaine's name had Rasheed clearing his throat and arching a pointed eyebrow at Ace from across the table. Ace subtly shook his head, not thinking it was the time. He knew he needed to be honest with Taj but didn't think a crowded bar was the place to do it.

"I really hate to hear that you two couldn't make it work but I guess you've gotta do what you've gotta do," Taj commented to Ricky, running a hand over his short locs. "You know what's best for you."

"I'm still gonna keep hope alive for you two, though," Rasheed added. "You never know how things can turn around."

Ricky scoffed. "Hmph."

"Hey, stranger things have happened."

"I guess." Ricky glanced at his watch. "I'm gonna head out, y'all. I've only let myself have one beer since I'm driving and I wanna get back to my room so I can drink myself to sleep."

"You sure? You can come hang out at my house, so you don't have to be by yourself in that hotel room," Taj offered.

"I appreciate it, brother, but I'm all right. And no offense, but you and Serenity aren't exactly fun to be around lately."

"Can't argue with you there," Taj muttered, snatching his jacket from the back of his chair.

Ricky and Taj stood, and Rasheed sent one more pointed glare to Ace, trying to get him to come clean. He was sick of being burdened with Ace's secrets, and he knew that the more time that passed, the less likely it was that Ace was going to confess everything. And even if he did, it would just make it worse that he waited so long.

When Ace kept his mouth shut and busied himself digging through his wallet for a tip, taking way longer than necessary for such a task, Rasheed felt his frustration snap. It was clear that Ace wasn't going to come clean on his own; he'd need to be forced into it. And maybe doing it in public would be better than in a private setting, where things were way more likely to go left.

"Ace has something he needs to say to you, Taj," Rasheed blurted just as they were getting their coats on. Ace's head snapped up, his eyes bulging in panic. "And it can't wait."

Taj and Ricky looked at Ace curiously while Ace wished he could slam Rasheed's head into the table. He knew he needed to let Taj know what happened between him and Serenity but he didn't appreciate being put on the spot. And he already knew that if he said anything other than the truth, Rasheed would probably just spill it himself, making Ace look even worse.

"What's up, man?" Taj asked Ace expectantly when a few quiet moments passed. "What's on your mind?"

Uncharacteristically nervous, Ace made himself stand from the table. His entire body was buzzing, like every nerve was exposed. His mind raced with what to say, knowing there was no smooth or slick way to tell Taj what he needed to tell him. It wasn't possible for him to spin this to where Taj wouldn't want to tear his head off, and he knew it.

"Umm, Taj, man, uh..." he stammered, his eyes pinging everywhere but at his friend. "I..."

"Damn, I've never seen you stumped like this," Ricky marveled. "You usually have something to say in any situation even when everyone else doesn't."

Clearing his throat, Ace rubbed the back of his neck so aggressively that his skin actually burned from the friction. He picked up his glass, but realized he'd drained it already and plunked it back down.

His friends waited while he tried to get himself together and gather the courage, and he finally made himself push some words out. "Something happened between...well, first, I know I never told you this, Taj, but Serenity and I kinda...have a past."

Taj's brows furrowed curiously. "What do you mean, a past? What kind of past?"

"We used to date. Back in the day."

"What?" Ricky exclaimed in surprise.

"We were like seventeen when we got together and only dated a couple of years; we even...I got her pregnant. But we lost the baby. Not too long after that, she dumped me."

All jaws were on the floor. Not even Rasheed knew about all of that.

"How come you never mentioned this before now?" Taj finally asked. "Hell, Serenity never said anything about it, either. What, did you two decide to keep it a secret? Does Charmaine know?"

"I haven't told Charmaine, either. It's not that it was a secret; we just figured it didn't matter since it was damn near twenty years ago and we had both moved on. Hell, we didn't even know y'all then. We didn't talk for years before we came back in touch, and by then I was with Charmaine. Then I introduced you and Serenity. We both figured it was a non-issue."

"Well, you were wrong," Taj snapped. "My woman being one of my boy's exes, a long time ago or not, is something I would've liked to have been informed of."

"Why, though? Would it have made any difference?"

"Maybe, maybe not. But I damn sure shouldn't have been kept in the dark about that. Charmaine, either. Especially since you two almost had a child together."

"I guess I didn't think about it like that," Ace muttering, wishing that was the extent of his confession. Taj already looked ticked off over what he'd told him, and it was by far the mildest of the things he needed to confess. Ace didn't know how Taj was going to react; Taj was usually the level-headed one, the peacemaker. The angriest Ace had seen Taj get was when he was fussing about how things were with Serenity on couple's night. He couldn't imagine what Taj would do once he heard everything.

"Well, you should've." Taj shook his head. "Wait, does this have anything to do with how Serenity has been acting lately? 'Cause she's feeling guilty about keeping that from me?"

Part of Ace wished he'd insisted they'd taken this conversation outside, because they were already drawing attention from people at nearby tables. He'd noticed a couple of curious glances being thrown their way, sensing the growing tension around them.

"Guilt has a lot to do with it," he made himself respond, "But that's not the part that has her so jacked up."

His eyes flitted to Rasheed, who nodded at him to keep going. Taj and Ricky each glanced at Rasheed, their curious frowns deepening. It was clear that Rasheed was already aware of whatever bombshell Ace was struggling to drop and that only made Taj more anxious and agitated.

"So what is it, then?" he asked impatiently.

"Yeah, what's going on?" Ricky asked, glancing at Rasheed again, who just held up his hands. He wasn't going to bail Ace out on this one.

Ace blew out a long breath. "You remember last year when Serenity went to that conference or whatever over in Brodence?"

Taj folded his arms. "Yeah. I think I was out of town myself at that time, visiting my parents."

"Right. So when her car broke down and she lost her wallet, she called me to come help her. By the time I got there and we got her car situation straightened out, it was really late and she was too tired to drive back. So I got her a hotel room."

The light of realization hit Ricky's eyes but he kept his mouth shut.

"She suggested I just stay with her and we both head back the next morning," Ace continued, now anxious to get everything out. He didn't realize how much it had been burdening him until he started to let go of it. "I figured, what the hell. Then we ordered shitty pizza and started drinking some wine that she had won at the conference, and got to talking. About random stuff, then about our respective relationships. Eventually that veered into how things ended up between us back in the day; I'd been carrying some resentment towards her over how she ended stuff, and things got pretty intense."

Taj stood there glaring at him with narrowed eyes, his face tightened in anger, his jaw clenched and his lips set in a hard line. Ace sensed that he already knew what was coming but was just waiting to hear him say it.

"Look, long story short..." Ace exhaled. "We kissed, and-"

"You kissed *her*?" Taj cut in, his voice sharp. "Or she kissed *you*?"

Momentarily stumped, Ace paused. "I don't remember exactly..."

"You can do better than that. Think harder."

Ace started to ask why it mattered either way, but thought better of it. He tried to remember the sequence of events from that night that he had spent so much time trying to block out. "She had started crying and I hugged her...I tried to calm her down and kissed her on the forehead...then she-she grabbed my face and kissed me. It just...kinda went on after that. Neither of us planned it-"

"But you let it happen, regardless."

"I...yeah." Ace's face was on fire.

"Uh-huh." Taj shifted his wide stance, his intense glare turning into lasers aimed straight at Ace's face. "And then what happened?"

All four men knew what happened next. But Taj wasn't going to let Ace off the hook by putting two and two together out loud. He wanted to hear him say it.

"It just escalated from there and we both lost our heads," Ace admitted. "I admit it; I wasn't thinking about my relationship at the time, with you or with Charmaine. It...I'm not proud of it, man. And it's been eating at me, though I tried to make myself forget about it. Once we both came down off the rush and the adrenaline and the alcohol, we both knew we had majorly fucked up."

"And just what did you *fuck up* doing?" Taj pressed. "Say what you did without dancing around it, Ace."

Ignoring the table next to them that wasn't even trying to hide that they were listening, Ace made himself say, "I slept with Serenity. And while I'm getting all this shit out, I might as well let you know that it happened again."

"What??" Rasheed exclaimed. He had no idea that Ace had cheated with Serenity a second time. "Are you fucking serious?"

Taj roughly snatched his chair out of the way and started to move towards Ace, but Ricky flung his arm out, stopping him and murmuring for him to keep it together. He could almost feel the heat radiating from his fuming friend and he too wished this wasn't happening in the middle of a bar.

"It was last week, when Serenity had come over 'cause she was upset about *you*," Ace informed, his voice tinged with the slightest bit of accusation. "She was all distraught over what you were doing when she got home and ran over to our house-"

"Wait, what the hell are you talking about?" Taj interjected. "What do you mean, what *I* was doing?"

"She said you were in there with some other woman."

"That's crazy!"

"Damn, Taj," Rasheed turned his incredulousness over to him. "Did you actually-"

"Hell no I didn't! And Serenity never said anything about that to me!"

"I didn't think it sounded right, either, but she insisted that's what she heard," Ace stated. "Charmaine had told her she could come over, then we got into an argument and she left. I was by myself with Serenity got there and told her she could come in and get her head together. I left her alone but she came in the den where I was and started bringing up that night last year, and how it was affecting her now, and she said something about wanting to feel better and asked me to kiss her. I told her no, but...I admit she wore me down. We ended up on the couch-"

"Gotdammit, Ace!" Ricky practically yelled, throwing his hands up.

"You are such a fucking idiot!" Rasheed shoved Ace in the shoulder, causing him to stumble several steps into the back of a nearby chair. "You let it happen *again*??"

Taj just stood there, eerily calm yet seething.

"Taj, man, I am so sorry!" Ace insisted. "I know I fucked up but it didn't mean anything! Serenity doesn't want me and I don't want her; she just wants you!"

"Wants me so much she kept giving it up to you while she shut me out, huh?" Taj growled.

"Man, the night last year...that was drunk nostalgia. Last week was some kind of revenge over what she thought *you* were doing."

"Even if that explains anything from her side, it doesn't explain why you gave in to her. What, were you getting revenge on Charmaine, too?"

Ace hunched his shoulders, having never considered that. "Maybe part of me was. She'd just threatened to leave me barely an hour before that and yeah, I was pissed. But man...if I could take it all back-"

"Yeah, but you can't. It's done." Taj started for Ace again but stopped himself right as Ricky grabbed his arm, forcing himself to take several deep breaths. His head was swimming and it felt like his heart was going to beat out of his chest. His hands tingled with wanting to rip Ace's face off, but he knew that when he finished doing that, his woman still would have cheated on him with friend. Twice. "I hope it was worth it. And I hope Charmaine leaves your trifling ass. You are fucking *dead* to me."

He turned and stormed towards the door, and Ricky was right on his heels after shooting one last angry glare at Ace.

Ace started after them. "Taj, come on, man-"

Rasheed yanked him back by the arm. "You need to keep your ass right here. Let him go."

"It wasn't like that; I swear it wasn't like that," Ace cried, almost to himself. He ran his hands down his face before pounding his fists on the table, making all the glasses jump. "Fuck!"

"Regardless, man, you boned your boy's woman," Rasheed reminded him, earning an angry glare from Ace. "There's no coming back from that."

Ace's eyes were on the floor as the reality of everything started to hit him. Taj now knew everything, and their friendship was likely done. He knew it would only be a matter of time before Charmaine found out, and the realization that he needed to confess all of this to her as well almost made the feeling go out of his legs. There was no doubt she'd leave him after this, and knowing that he'd messed up two relationships that were important to him made his chest pound with regret.

His hand blindly groped for the nearest chair and he sank down onto it, fully aware that he was being filmed by nosy bystanders but not caring. It didn't even matter. Even if nobody else had been around to witness it, he'd still made yet another mess that he knew he wouldn't be able to clean up.

Chapter 13

Lavinia & Ricky

It had been two weeks and Ricky still hadn't gone home or acknowledged any of Lavinia's messages. Every day she came home from work, she expected to see the rest of his things moved out and always breathed a sigh of relief when she saw them still there.

"This is a long time for your husband to be gone," her mother Darla commented one evening. She was supposed to have gone back home already but insisted on staying when Ricky made himself scarce, and for once, Lavinia regretted inviting her there. She wanted to be alone. "You think he's with another woman?"

Lavinia didn't. Regardless of what she might've insinuated to her mother, she never believed Ricky was cheating on her. That wasn't the kind of man he was.

"No," she replied in a low voice, pulling at the frayed edge in one of the holes in her distressed jeans. "I don't."

"Where else would he be, then? No man just up and leaves his wife for no reason. I know you said that he was mad and jealous of you and how well you're doing. You think that's what it is, still? I see why you called him a punk."

Wincing at those words, Lavinia squeezed her eyes shut. Hearing someone talk about her husband that way burned her. Even more so because she knew she'd planted that seed herself, despite knowing better. Ricky was anything but a punk, nor was he weak. She'd known that when she was saying it that day, but she let the words come out, anyway. It was easier to call him that than face the fact that her husband needed therapy just to stay in the same house with her.

"Ricky didn't want you to stay with us," she finally admitted. She glanced up at Darla. "He told me that he didn't think it was a good idea and I didn't listen to him."

"Hmm." Darla moved over to the loveseat across from where Lavinia sat, the mug full of spiked coffee between her hands. "And why didn't you listen to him?"

Hunching a shoulder, Lavinia's hands eased into her lap, disappearing between her thick thighs. "It was what I wanted. And I admit I've gotten used to getting my way around here. Ricky doesn't like conflict and I know it's because of how his parents used to fuss and fight all the time, even to the point of getting physical. And I learned pretty early on that if I bugged him about something long enough, he'd give in just to keep the peace."

"So you took advantage of him."

Her head snapping up, Lavinia immediately started to protest. "What? No!"

"Yes, you did." Darla crossed her legs and tucked some hair behind her ear. "You used what you knew about him and his past to get what you wanted. There's no other way to slice it."

"I...that's not what I was trying to do, though!"

"I bet it was. You've *always* wanted to get your way and would pitch a fit whenever somebody told you no. I blame your daddy for that, 'cause he spoiled you rotten, giving you every damn thing you asked for, even overriding me and telling you yes when I had already said no. And now you apparently expect your husband to treat you the same way."

Lavinia frowned. She'd never thought of things that way. In her mind, her father was simply showing her how she deserved to be treated. It wasn't a bad thing.

But clearly, it couldn't have been that good since her husband now refused to come home.

"Look, I just know what I want," she defended, not wanting to acknowledge her mother's point. "I was strong-willed when Ricky met me; this isn't anything new. I don't know why he's tripping now."

Darla sipped her coffee. "Of course you don't."

"This isn't all on me. A marriage takes two people."

"Yeah. It also takes two people to acknowledge what's wrong and fix it. Sounds like he's been trying to do that by going to therapy. So what have *you* done?"

"I..." Lavinia's voice faded out, knowing her mother would see through any lie she'd try to tell right then. Darla waited with an arched brow. "I'm...damn, whose side are you on?"

"You never were good at admitting when you were wrong. I blame your damn daddy for that, too, 'cause he was always making excuses for you and letting you off the hook for stuff. Part of me wanted to warn Ricky before y'all got married."

"Thanks a lot, Mama."

Lavinia grabbed the remote and turned on the television, needing to be done with this conversation. So her father had spoiled her, so what? That didn't make her a bad person. And Ricky didn't used to mind indulging her and making her happy. He's the one who changed over the years; not her.

And during the first year of their marriage, they made a promise to each other that they'd work out whatever came up between them, no matter how bad it was. So Ricky would *have* to come home and work this out at some point. He'd always been a man of his word.

The more she forced those kinds of thoughts through her mind, the better she felt. She absolutely wanted her man at home, but if some time away from her was what he needed to get his head together so they could start trying to work through this tough time they were in, then so be it.

He'll come around, she silently assured herself, tucking her legs underneath her on the couch and avoiding her mother's knowing look. *He has to.*

"Thank you for making some time for me today, Ms. Hyman."

Lavinia looked up from the paperwork on her desk with an arched brow. Her client, Porter Abrams, sat across from her with a smirk, his eyes dipping to her cleavage as it already had several times since he sat down.

"It's *Mrs.* Hyman," she corrected him, pointedly flipping a page with her left hand and flashing her wedding ring. "As I believe I've informed you already."

"My mistake. No disrespect intended. I guess my wishful thinking is getting the best of me, that's all."

Choosing not to acknowledge his statement, Lavinia turned her attention back to the paperwork on her desk. "So as I mentioned on the phone, everything looked good with the extra inspections you requested, outside of the issues you were already aware of. But the seller did come back with a counteroffer."

"What?" Porter frowned. "The offer I made them was more than fair."

"I agree, but it's up to them whether they'll accept or not. And your offer was ten thousand below asking."

"Because the house is damn near thirty years old and has a bad roof, not to mention the other work I'd need to do to it before I could move in."

"I understand that, Mr. Abrams-"

"Porter," he interjected, sitting forward in his seat as his frown melted. "I've asked you to call me Porter."

"Fine, Porter. I get what you're saying and I agree with you. I can go back to them with another offer, stressing the improvements the house still needs. Not to mention, it's been on the market for almost a year."

"Which is exactly why I requested another inspection. I figured there had to be something wrong with it to be on the market so long, but to my surprise, it wasn't anything we didn't already know about."

"The sellers are just stubborn and don't want to budge on their asking price, but let me try to work my magic; I'll get them to see reason," Lavinia assured, closing the folder on her desk and smiling at him. "I'll give them a call later this afternoon."

"I have faith in you, Mrs. Hyman." Porter's eyes roamed over her appreciatively yet again as his fingertips stroked his clean-shaven brown chin, and she tried to keep her expression neutral, despite her growing annoyance. "Or, Lavinia."

"Mrs. Hyman is fine."

"We've been working together for a minute now; I don't see why we have to be so formal. Are you this stiff with all your other clients?"

Her face tightening, Lavinia stood, pulling down her tight mid-thigh-length skirt before turning towards the door. "I'm not stiff. But seeing as how you've made it more than clear that your interest in me isn't totally professional, we need to keep *some* level of boundary, here."

"I see." Porter stood, smoothly buttoning his suit jacket before meeting her at her office door. He looked down at her as she stood with her hand on the knob, eying him. His hands eased behind his back as he cocked his head to the side, biting his lower lip. "I didn't think you minded that, my personal interest in you."

She frowned. "And why is that?"

He stepped closer, and since her stubbornness wouldn't let her step back and seem like she was retreating, she stayed in place and let his chest lightly touch hers. "Because you always seem like you're happy to see me. You mean to tell me you don't wear outfits like this to get my attention? You're offering up the goods and..." He licked his lips. "I'm more than happy to indulge."

His eyes fell to her protruding breasts again, and she had to resist the strong urge to knee him in the balls. She was in the perfect position for it. And with the way he was acting, she would be totally justified.

Instead, though, she placed a hand to his chest and gave it a hard push, sending him back a couple of steps. "My clothes aren't an indication of anything other than being what I like to wear. Even if I came up in here in a string bikini, that doesn't give you the right to proposition me. I have no problem referring you to another agent if this is going to continue being a problem. Trust me, it'll be your loss more than mine, because nobody in this office is a good as I am."

Porter's grunt was automatic. "I don't doubt that."

Stepping closer, Lavinia looked up straight into his milky brown eyes, lowering her voice. "Believe me, I know I look damn good. And I don't care if you want me; you should. But I'm a married woman. So keep your comments to yourself. Because trust me, eye-fucking is as close as you're gonna get." She arched a brow at his sharp intake of breath. "Are we in agreement?"

He started to respond, but stopped himself. Lavinia could only imagine what he'd been about to say.

"All right, then," he conceded, holding up his hands. "Agreed."

"Good." She stepped back and opened the door. "I'll give you a call after I speak with the sellers."

"I'll look forward to it." Porter paused as he passed by her, leaning down slightly. "And thanks for the string bikini visual. I'll be using that later."

He strode out of the office before she could respond, and Lavinia just rolled her eyes and closed the door, shaking off the encounter.

She got back to work, but wasn't able to let go of her annoyance at the whole scene with Porter. He certainly wasn't the first client to hit on her, and she usually enjoyed the attention, even if she never indulged. But for whatever reason, this time rubbed her the wrong way. Maybe because Porter dared to imply that the way she dressed gave him a free pass to ogle her. As far as Lavinia was concerned, it didn't matter how much cleavage or legs she showed, she still deserved respect.

When she went to the break room for another cup of coffee an hour or so later, she was still internally fuming. She almost didn't even notice her coworker Kelis come in.

"What's wrong, Lavinia?"

Startled, Lavinia put down the bottle of French vanilla creamer she'd been holding. "What do you mean?"

"You're frowning."

"Oh." Yanking a stirring straw from the holder, she swirled it inside her steaming coffee as she leaned a hip against the counter. "Guess I'm still thinking about the frustrating meeting I had a little while ago."

"What happened?"

"That Porter Abrams. He's gotten a little too comfortable with me."

Kelis frowned curiously, rounding the table in the middle of the room towards Lavinia. "What do you mean?"

"He flirts too much. And has made it clear that he'd like things to go past the professional with me. The bastard couldn't keep his damn eyes off my chest the whole time he was in my office."

Her face clearing, Kelis ran a hand through her mahogany bobbed hair. "Oh."

"He actually said that he thought I *wanted* him to do all that, because of how I dress. Can you believe that?"

Clearing her throat, Kelis's eyes flew towards the ceiling.

Lavinia put down her coffee cup. "What?"

"Lavinia...look, you and I have worked together for a while now. And true enough, he had no right to come at you like that, but-"

"*But??*"

"Well, you *do* dress rather inappropriately for the office," Kelis told her. "There's nothing wrong with being proud of your body and looking good, but, damn, girl." She motioned towards Lavinia's chest. "Those things are *always* hanging out. It's hard *not* to look at them."

Lavinia's jaw dropped. She hadn't expected that. "So, what, this is something that has been talked about behind my back?"

"It's been brought up, yeah," Kelis admitted. "More than a few times. But I guess no one confronted you about it since you always handle your business and it hasn't presented a problem yet, business-wise. But if clients are coming on to you because of it-"

"It's *their* problem, not mine," Lavinia interjected. "I'm not doing anything wrong. These are supposed to be grown men we're dealing with; it's not my fault they can't keep their dicks from getting hard just because they're around a sexy, voluptuous, confident woman."

Kelis's brown skin flushed slightly as she held up her hands. "Hey, don't snap at me. I'm not the boss around here; I don't care what you wear. I'm just letting you know that it's not just Mr. Abrams's attention that you're catching with all that. Do what you do, just...be careful. That's all I'm saying."

Lavinia's eyes narrowed slightly as Kelis went to remove a brown paper bag from the refrigerator before leaving the break room. So her coworkers were talking about her behind her back too, huh?

"Fuck them," she muttered to herself, picking her coffee back up. She refused to change how she was just because a few people didn't like it, or because some men wanted to act like they'd never seen a set of titties before. She was there to sell houses, that's it. It wasn't her fault that people wanted to pay so much attention to the clothes she chose to wear.

As she headed back to her office, though, she was even more aware of what people might've been thinking as they gave her pleasantries as she passed. She could only imagine what was probably said about her in private conversations. As if any of them were perfect. If Lavinia wanted to be petty, she could say something about everyone in that office, including Kelis.

But as she shut the door to her office and went back to her desk, she reminded herself that it didn't matter what anyone thought. Her daddy had always told her that she should be proud of her beauty and her body, and that anyone that had an issue with that was just jealous.

"Kelis's skinny ass *wishes* she had these boobs," she muttered to herself, actually caressing them as she checked her calendar. She had another client meeting to prepare for and didn't have time for this foolishness.

Her mind suddenly flashed back to a couple years earlier when she was showing a house to a couple that was planning to move to town. She remembered what she was wearing that day; a cranberry vest and skirt set that hugged her body, and four-inch multicolored heels. The wife had gone to the bathroom for the third time thanks to her advanced pregnancy, and Lavinia had wandered over to the bay window in the spacious living room to check a message on her phone. Suddenly she felt hands slide underneath her arms and grab her breasts, and a hard dick press against her backside. She'd gasped and whirled around, but before she could go off, the husband grabbed the back of her head and kissed her forcefully, jamming his tongue into her mouth as he backed her against the wall. Lavinia's phone fell to the hardwood floor as she tried to push him away, her protests swallowed by his probing kisses. She remembered the fear and anger coursing through her as this man who had seemed so respectable and polite grinding against her while his pregnant wife was just a couple rooms away.

"Meet me tonight," he had whispered, working his hands underneath her skirt as he eyed her hungrily. "Then we can give each other what we both want. She goes to bed early and sleeps like a log; she won't even know-"

"Get the fuck off me!" Lavinia had screeched, managing to push him away and slap him across the face. She fumed in anger at his gall, her chest heaving. "How dare you-"

"How dare I *what*?" His voice had hardened as he looked at her with razor-sharp eyes. "Accept what you've been offering? You've been flirting with me since the first meeting, *Mrs. Hyman*, and you damn know it. Any time my wife's back was turned, you were giving me these sly smiles and winking and pushing your chest in my face. You gonna try to deny that?"

Lavinia sobered, hating that there was some truth to his words. She *did* tend to flirt with male clients to get the deal, and it didn't always matter if they were with significant others or not. To her, it was all harmless; a sales tactic. She never intended for it to go any further than that. Lavinia was used to the men flirting back, but actually grabbing and kissing her? That was a first, and it didn't make her feel good.

She ended up losing the sale that day when the husband suddenly claimed he didn't like the house, then ultimately convinced his wife they needed to find another agent. Lavinia had been too embarrassed to tell anyone what really happened, even her girls. There was no way she could tell Ricky. At least it hadn't gone further than it did, though Lavinia hated to think what might have happened if she'd been in the house alone with that handsy creep. She'd managed to force that whole scene from her mind, practically convincing herself it didn't happen while simultaneously vowing to be more careful in the future.

Now, Lavinia thought back to Ricky's past admonishment about her work outfits and questioning if she was trying to entice clients with her body. She recalled her girls occasionally warning her over the years about how her intentions could be misinterpreted. Mr. Abrams lusty eyes that couldn't stay off her breasts. Kelis's revelations about how her associates perceived her.

Lavinia's stubbornness wanted to dismiss everyone and declare them all wrong. But she couldn't.

It hit her that maybe her way wasn't always the best way, regardless of her intentions. And if she was wrong about this, maybe she'd been wrong about other things, too, including how she handled things in her marriage.

She dropped the pen she'd been holding and put her head in her hands, wondering how her life had gotten to be such a mess.

Hours later, Lavinia headed home. She'd hoped that she'd finally hear back from Ricky, but yet another day had passed with no contact. She was trying to be patient and let him work through what he needed to work through, but it was getting hard to keep her game face on. The fact that Ricky had stayed out of their house for so long and ignored all of her messages gave her a bad feeling. He wasn't even trying to placate her or give her any kind of indication of where he was with everything. He was just leaving her in the dark, which Lavinia hated. Things being so up in the air was torture for her. She just wanted her husband to come home so they could start getting past this bump in the road.

When she pulled up at the house and saw his truck outside, she literally squealed with joy, feeling like her prayers were finally being answered. She actually double-checked to make sure it was their house, and that it was Ricky's truck. Her hopes were sky-high as she screeched her car into the driveway next to his Tahoe and hurried out of the car, forgetting her purse as she made a beeline for the door. The anticipation of seeing her husband only made her realize how much she really did miss him while he was gone, and she told herself to watch what she said when she saw him; the last thing she wanted was more arguments. She wouldn't even drill him about where he'd been or why he'd shut her out like he had. There would be time for explanations later; for now, she just wanted to throw her arms around him and give him a fitting welcome home.

She could hear him upstairs when she entered the house, and she stopped in the downstairs guest bathroom to check her hair and freshen her makeup, though that was when she realized she'd left her purse in the car. Figuring she didn't need it, she just ran her hands through her long silky black hair extensions and smoothed out her clothing, adjusting her low-cut top and hiking her skirt up another inch or so. Her hands were actually shaking, and she blew out a breath to calm herself. This was her husband that she'd been with for years; there was no reason to be so nervous. She just didn't want to say the wrong thing and send him running again.

At least her mother had left, finally. So she and Ricky could reconcile and talk in private. And if Lavinia was honest with herself, she hoped Ricky would be willing to do more than talk; they hadn't made love since couple's night. She was long overdue and needed Ricky's body on hers, even if he was still a little miffed at her.

Finally feeling she was ready, she exited the bathroom and headed for the stairs. Part of her wished Ricky would have come downstairs to greet her, since she figured he'd heard her come in, but she told herself it wasn't important. If what he needed was for her to make the first move, then so be it. Excitement buzzed through her body and her smile grew the closer she got to their bedroom.

But that smile faded when she pushed open the door and saw their king-sized bed covered with suitcases, and her husband standing next to it with empty eyes.

"Ricky..." She stepped further into the room, looking at all of the suitcases. One glance at the closet confirmed he'd cleared most of his things out. "What's going on?"

"I'm leaving." His voice was flat as he pressed a pair of neatly folded jeans into the suitcase in front of him. "For good this time."

Chapter 14

Charmaine & Ace

"Take it, Ace."

"No!"

"You might as well. There's no need for me to keep it anymore, at this point."

Ace continued to adamantly shake his head, backing away from the engagement ring that Charmaine was holding out to him. They'd finally had it out after Ace got home from Fourth and Long, when he confessed his transgressions to Taj. Charmaine had been home waiting for him and she confronted him about what Serenity revealed to her (after she threw a shoe at him as soon as he walked through the door). She screamed at him, and he took it for a while before his frustration overflowed and he started yelling back at her. They'd gone at it so long that they exhausted themselves too much to resolve anything that night.

But now it was the next day and Charmaine was trying to give her engagement ring back to him, and Ace was having none of it.

"You didn't seriously think we'd still be getting married after this, did you?" she asked him, the ring still resting in her extended palm. "You cheated on me, Ace. Twice!"

"And I'm sorry about that, Charmaine; more than I can tell you. And crazy or not, I still want us to try to work this out."

"Are you nuts? You slept with my friend right there on that very couch and you think there's still something to work out?"

"Babe..." Ace dropped onto the couch, staying away from the spot where Serenity had ridden him mere nights before, "You have no idea how much I wish I could take all that back. I love you more than anything."

"Don't tell me you love me more than anything." Charmaine stuffed her hands under her arms, frowning. "Not when you could let yourself sleep with another woman."

"Look, I know it's cliché, but it was just sex; it didn't mean shit," Ace insisted. "As soon as it was over, I wished I could've gone back and been stronger about not letting Serenity get to me. I don't want her, babe; I just want you. And that's on everything."

"Whatever, Ace. Regardless, you apparently can't keep it in your damn pants if someone tempts you enough. I'm not going into a marriage with somebody like that. Hell, I'm not staying a relationship at all with someone like that."

"It's not like Serenity is the first woman to push up on me. A bunch of women have tried to come at me and I didn't even give them the time of day."

"You expect praise for this?"

"All I'm saying is that what went down with Serenity was just because of all of our history and whatever unresolved issues we still had," Ace explained, looking up at her with pleading eyes. "I thought we were past all that shit, but I realized I'd been suppressing a bunch of stuff over the years. It doesn't mean I don't still want to be with you. I..." He sighed, dropping his head as his hand ran over his hair, "Whatever I've gotta do to prove that it's you and only you that I want, I'll do it. I can't lose you, Charmaine. Please..."

Charmaine hated that she was affected by his words, but she was. She'd been prepared to call off their engagement and their relationship and start the process of dividing their things. It was Ace's house, so she was planning to start looking for another place to live; Iman had already told her she could crash at her place while she looked.

But seeing how contrite Ace was and hearing the conviction in his voice was keeping her feet planted in place and the engagement ring pressing into her balled fist. Her head told her to just throw it and run, but she couldn't.

Maybe because her heart was reminding her that Ace wasn't the only one in the wrong.

Amongst the shock and anger upon hearing about Ace and Serenity, Charmaine had temporarily forgotten about her own indiscretions. And even before that, she knew she hadn't been very pleasant to live with. As wrong as Ace was for giving in to Serenity, she had felt pricked when he'd admitted that her hasty ultimatum was part of the reason he'd been so angry and out-of-his-head that night.

"Damn it," she whispered, dropping her arms. She took a seat on the ottoman and looked at the carpeted floor for several moments before turning her eyes to him. "Is there anything else I need to know, Ace? Even if you might not think it's significant, are there *any* other secrets or mistakes that you're keeping from me?"

"No," he immediately replied, shaking his head. "This was everything, I *swear*."

Choosing to believe him, Charmaine pursed her lips. Her fingers pressed into the ring in her hand. "In that case, there's something I need to admit to you, too."

Sitting up, Ace's dark brows furrowed slightly. "What?"

"Before I tell you this, just know it doesn't absolve you of anything. And I still don't know if we need to be together, given everything that's happened. But it's only fair that we both be honest and get everything out on the table."

His frown deepened. "What is it, Charmaine?"

"I made out with somebody else not too long ago."

Ace blinked, almost as if her words didn't register. "Say what?"

"I kissed someone else. Actually, if I'm real about it, it was a little more than just kissing," Charmaine admitted, her eyes on his. "But that's as far as it went. I'm not proud of it, but-"

"Wait a minute. So you blew up at me for stepping out on you when you knew you had already cheated on me your damn self?"

"*I* didn't sleep with anybody, Ace," Charmaine insisted, poking a finger to her chest. "It was just some kissing and petting and-"

"Cheating," Ace grunted. "It's still cheating, Charmaine, and you know it."

"You still cheated worse. And *twice*."

"Seriously? So that's what we're doing now, huh? You get to mess up and still get let off the hook because you didn't go as far as I did?"

"Ace...no, that's not what I'm saying," Charmaine conceded with a sigh. "Regardless of what we each did, we were *both* wrong for going outside of our relationship. I get that."

Trying to tell himself to calm down, Ace scrubbed his hands over his face and took a few deep breaths. The thought of Charmaine with another man was making his blood boil but he had to check himself. "Who was it?"

"Ace, I don't think it's important to-"

"Who was it, Charmaine??"

"*Ugh*! It was Tango!"

His head snapped up. "Tango from the bakery? *That* Tango??"

Charmaine mindlessly turned the ring around in her fingers. "Yeah. That Tango."

"So..." Ace's head was spinning. No *wonder* she was always up at that bakery; those butter yellow boxes had become a staple in their house. He never would have guessed that it was about more than her love of cupcakes. "How did this happen? *When* did this happen??"

Charmaine wasn't eager to go into all the details but knew it was only fair that she did. "If I'm honest about it, we'd been doing some mild flirting for a while, but I never planned on anything coming of it. I don't remember the exact day now, but not too long after couple's night, I went there and we got to talking, and somehow I let myself start venting about you. I started crying, he comforted me and...we kissed. But it was just a peck...I stopped it and left."

"I thought you said it was just that one time. Where does all the petting and shit come in, if it was 'just a peck'?"

"I wasn't really counting this time as anything-"

"I don't know why not. You would have if it were me."

"Okay, fine. I'll own that. So, the night we had that last fight and I left, I went to Pure Sugar."

"To see him?"

"Just to stuff my face. I was actually hoping to talk to Peaches but she was out; it was just Tango there. It was almost closing time, and I just hung around, helping get things cleaned up while we talked about random whatever. Then he locked the doors and invited me to watch television in the office. Somehow I ended up on his lap."

Ace felt his anger surge and everything in him wanted to grab his keys and go straight over to Pure Sugar and push Tango's head into a heavy-duty mixer while it was running. But he knew that wouldn't change anything.

"And what else?" he made himself ask, not wanting to hear any more but still needing to know everything.

"We were making out in the desk chair," Charmaine informed, her eyes averted. "I let him take my shirt off, he took his off...there was grinding, some licking, but that's it. When he unbuttoned my pants and had me grab his dick, that woke me up and I realized just what I was doing. That's also when I remembered Serenity was coming over. So I grabbed my shirt and got the hell out of there."

"So while I was here with her, you were there with him."

"Yeah." She made herself return his hard glare. "Pretty much."

"So we *both* fucked up. It wasn't just me."

She automatically started to protest, but stopped herself. "No, Ace, it wasn't just you."

They sat in silence for several moments, each stewing over the recent revelations. Ace couldn't believe Charmaine had stepped out on him. He'd always thought she was above stuff like that, probably because she always acted like she was. She was always getting onto him about everything, acting like she was the adult in the relationship; it was throwing him for a loop that she had screwed up so royally, herself.

But he knew he had no room to feel relieved. Charmaine messing up didn't mean he was in the clear. He was wrong to ever touch Serenity, and he'd had given anything to go back and make better decisions.

Part of him wondered if Charmaine was as remorseful about her little session with Tango.

"So what happens now?" he finally asked, his voice low.

She sighed. "I don't know."

"I'm pissed about what you just told me, Charmaine. But I still don't want to lose you. I still want us to work through this."

Giving a sarcastic chuckle, Charmaine shot him an incredulous look. "And how are we supposed to do that, Ace? After all this?"

"I don't know. We can go to counseling or something."

"Oh, *now* you want to go to counseling?"

"I said I was willing to do whatever it took and I meant it. Clearly, we both have some issues. And I'm willing to work on mine. Even after hearing about the shit you did, I'm not willing to just walk away from us, Charmaine. I still want this."

Her eyes softened at his words. As angry as she still was at Ace for what he did with Serenity, she still loved him. And he wasn't the only one who had made mistakes. She couldn't even say her little makeout session with Tango was in the name of revenge, because she hadn't known about what Ace did yet. She'd just been wrong. Regardless of how frustrated she was with Ace and how unsure she might've been about their relationship, the fact was they were still engaged while she went and got intimate with another man. There was no excusing that.

And if she was honest with herself, she didn't want to lose Ace, either.

"We can talk about that," she finally responded. "If you're *really* serious about everything you just said-"

"I'm dead-ass," he insisted. "Whatever I gotta do, babe."

"All right. We can give it a try, then."

"I'm glad to hear you say that. And whether or not you wanna hear it right now or choose to believe me, I'm gonna go ahead and tell you that you absolutely won't have to worry about anything like this happening again, with Serenity or anybody else. That shit with her is in the past. It's just me and you. And I put that on my *life*."

There wasn't a hint of amusement on his face. Charmaine heard the conviction in his voice, and knew he meant what he was saying. As crazy as it sounded, maybe they had a chance, after all.

"And I'll go somewhere else when I want some cupcakes," she assured him. "You don't have to worry about anything else happening with me and Tango, or anyone else. And I'm sorry for letting that happen, Ace. For real."

"I'm sorry, too." He stood, tentatively reaching for her hand. She let him pull her up and slide his arms around her. "I know shit with our friends is fucked up but I'm glad we still have each other, babe. I swear I'm not gonna mess this up again."

"Let's not make any big promises right now, Ace," she suggested, running her hands along his dark arms. "Let's crawl before we try to run."

"Damn that, I'm *runnin'*," Ace insisted, his hold on her tightening. He leaned down and rubbed his cheek against hers. "All I have to do is remember you standing here trying to give me that engagement ring back and that's all the incentive I need to keep my ass in line. Shit got extra real when you took that off. Speaking of which, can you please put it back on now?"

"On one condition."

"What? Name it."

"We need to get rid of that damn couch."

"I don't know if I'm more floored or glad that you and Ace are staying together after what he did," Iman told Charmaine a couple of days later. They were at her place, after Charmaine had asked if she could come by after work. "I thought you'd be here with all your bags the night you found out about everything."

"That was the plan. But Ace wasn't the only one who messed up. I was just as wrong for fooling around with Tango, regardless of whether we went all the way or not."

"Oh, I'm still tripping about that, too, believe me." Iman grabbed a couple of bottles of water and some hot Cheetos from the kitchen and padded back over to the couch, the pink polish on her toenails shining. Charmaine had never been jealous of anyone's feet before she saw Iman's. "No wonder you were always going to that bakery. Ain't nobody's cupcakes *that* good."

"Hush, Iman."

"For real, though, I didn't even know you were into Tango like that. I mean, buddy is fine as hell, but still."

"He was more of a fantasy, really. To be honest, it kinda blew my mind when he started flirting with me; I didn't think I'd be his type. Stepping out on Ace wasn't anything I planned and it's certainly not anything I'm proud of."

"I know, girl. You know I won't judge. And if working things out with Ace is what you want and feel is right, then I'm happy for you."

"I appreciate it. As jacked up as things are and despite everything that's happened, I think Ace and I can find our way through all this. We're gonna start going to couple's counseling next week; we're doing virtual sessions with this doctor in Brodence that came highly recommended."

"After how he laughed in your face when you mentioned it before?" Iman opened the bag of hot Cheetos and put it between them on the couch. "He must really mean business."

"I think he does. And I do, too. It wasn't all on him."

"So you're willing to forgive *him*...what about Serenity?"

Charmaine paused in opening her bottle of water. "What *about* Serenity?"

"You know what I mean. Are you gonna forgive her, too?"

"I honestly haven't given it much thought, since I've been so focused on me and Ace. But as of right now, I doubt it."

Iman peered at her for a few moments before turning her eyes to the episode of *Grey's Anatomy* that was playing on the television. "I see."

"You disagree, I take it?"

"Doesn't matter what I think. It's totally your decision."

"Don't do that, Iman. We're closer than that. I'm asking you what you think."

"I could see it either way, honestly. I'd get it if you were done with her but I'd also understand if you were willing to try to forgive her, especially if she's sincerely sorry. Has she tried to call?"

"Like ten times."

"She was absolutely wrong for what she did. But she did confess everything, and *before* Ace did, I might add. Even if she has to earn your trust back, it wouldn't be the craziest thing in the world to try to work things out with her."

Charmaine looked at her thoughtfully. "I'm kinda surprised to hear you say that."

"Girl...you know I've been through some shit in the past. Life is just too short to not forgive. Not even for her sake, but for yours." She popped a Cheeto into her mouth. "But like I said, it's your decision."

Charmaine pondered her friend's words. She hadn't given much thought to how she'd handle her mangled friendship with Serenity, or if she even wanted to. It was one thing to forgive Ace, but knowing that her friend had come onto her man was something else. Charmaine wasn't sure she could get past that, even if she wanted to.

"I don't know," she finally huffed, shaking the subject off. "I don't want to think about her right now. There's actually a reason I wanted to come by to see you tonight."

Iman looked over at her, eyebrows lifted in curiosity. "What's that?"

"I want you to give me a makeover."

"What? Why?"

"It's just something I feel is necessary."

"How is that necessary, Charmaine? There's nothing wrong with you the way you are."

"I know that, but-"

"And you *better* not be saying that how you look or dress has anything to do with what Ace did," Iman demanded. "'Cause if you are, I'll knock you into next week."

"Will you calm down? This is not about Ace. I want to do this for myself. I feel like I'm entering a new chapter in my life and I just want to change up my look some, that's all. I'm just talking about changing my hair and getting some cuter clothes, and finding the right shade of lipstick; I've never been good at that. It's not like I'm about to go out and get a butt implant."

Calming down, Iman's frown eased. "Oh."

"So will you help me?"

"Yeah, girl, of course. You know I love to spruce myself up. We can do it this weekend; we'll make a day of it."

"Thank you! You think we should invite Lavinia?"

"Ehh. We can, but I doubt she'll be up for it. If Ricky was serious about leaving her like Rasheed said he was, then I doubt she'll be worried about getting her hair done."

"What?" Charmaine gasped. "Ricky is actually going to leave her?"

"According to Rasheed, yeah. Ricky was pretty adamant about it, he said. I tried to go by and see her at her office during my lunch hour today but they said she didn't come in, and she wasn't answering my calls. I can only imagine shit has finally hit the fan over there."

"Oh my god," Charmaine sunk against the back of the couch. "I knew things were rough between her and Ricky but I never expected him to actually *leave*."

"I hate to say it but I'm not all that surprised. You've heard how she talks to him, and I can only imagine that it's worse when they're alone. And Ricky has been looking miserable for a while now; guess he's finally reached his breaking point."

"I'm gonna think positively. If me and Ace can work things out, maybe they can, too."

"Anything is possible, I guess."

"And speaking of you and Rasheed..."

"What the hell? We *weren't* speaking of me and Rasheed."

"Well, we are now."

"Let's not." Iman held up a hand before stuffing her mouth with more Cheetos. "I don't have the energy."

"Why is it you have so much to say about everything else but you wanna clam up when it gets to be about you?"

"Me and Rasheed..." Iman sighed, letting her head fall against the back of the couch. "I decided that we're better off as friends."

"Why? I thought you were in love with him."

"I said I *might* be in love with him. And even if I was, I don't know how he feels about me and I've been too much of a punk to ask. I just keep hearing him tell me that I'm doing too much and all this was a mistake. I can't take that rejection; not from him. That's why I've been semi-avoiding him whenever he's called to hook up, and I can only imagine he's probably ticked at me about that. So we should just leave well enough alone before we start resenting each other altogether."

"Uh-huh. And you'll be okay with that?"

Iman hunched a shoulder. "I'll learn to live with it."

"Iman." Charmaine waited for her friend to finally look at her. "You and I both know that if you stop this thing between you and Rasheed before really seeing where it could go, you'll be miserable. Don't do that to yourself, or to him, if you don't need to. Remember what you said earlier about life being too short? You're not exempt from that, girl."

Knowing there was nothing she could say to dispute that, Iman just turned her glassy eyes back to the television.

Chapter 15

Serenity & Taj

Fear ripped through Serenity as she stared at Taj standing in the door to her office at the café. He looked angrier than she'd ever seen him and she immediately knew that he'd found out about her and Ace.

"How long did you think you could avoid me?" he asked, his voice gruff. "I'm not gonna bother asking where you slept last night, since you didn't have the guts to come home and face me."

"Can you come in and close the door?" she requested, trying to keep the shakiness out of her voice. "I'd rather everyone not hear our business."

Pursing his lips, Taj obliged, resisting the urge to slam the door like he wanted to. He would've preferred to have this showdown in a more private setting, but since Serenity had been keeping her distance the last couple of days, he had no choice but to corner her at work.

"You wanna sit down?" Serenity asked him. "I can get you a latte or-"

"How 'bout we get right to the part where you tell me how long you planned on keeping me in the dark about you and Ace?"

She winced slightly. "There *is* no 'me and Ace', Taj. What happened between us...it's in the past."

"The past being what, a week or two ago? Don't act like it's been years and years since you went to his house and seduced him."

Tears were already pricking her eyes but Serenity fought to keep them at bay. "Taj...I make no excuses for that. But for the record, I didn't go there to seduce him; I went to see Charmaine after I found out about you and that other woman."

"Yeah, about that." Taj folded his arms over his chest. "Where did you get the idea that I cheated on you?"

"From my own ears, Taj. I heard you."

"You heard *what*? You are the only woman I've been with in any way, shape or form since we got together, Serenity. So don't try to make yourself less guilty by dragging me into it."

"I'm not!" Serenity stood from her desk, some of her anger returning. The sounds of Taj and that woman through their bedroom door had haunted her almost as hard as the memory of her and Ace on his couch. She'd been in her own private hell for weeks, and she was willing to own up to her part in things, but it annoyed her that Taj wasn't willing to do the same. "Taj, the night I told you I was working late, I came home wanting to finally own up to things and start working through our issues, and I heard all the moaning through the door. *And* the door was locked. It was clearly your voice and another woman's. Please don't insult me by trying to tell me I didn't hear anything when I know I did."

Realization washed over Taj's face and his eyes closed momentarily, shaking his head. Things made a little more sense now, though his anger barely dissipated. "So that's what this was about? Some tit for tat?"

"Like I said, Taj, I went to talk to Charmaine, not to see Ace. I didn't know she had left. And I only went in anyway because I'd been drinking and didn't think it would be smart to drive anywhere else. Yes, I came onto Ace and I own that. It's just...when I thought about you and that woman-"

"There was no woman, Serenity. I was in the room alone."

She sighed. "Taj, I'm trying to be honest with you. I need you to do the same for me."

"I'm being honest. I was watching porn."

It was as if someone splashed her with ice cold water. "Wh-what?"

"Porn, Serenity. Something I've had to resort to more and more lately since our sex life has gone down the tubes. You know, since you cheated on me the *first* time when you were out of town?"

Serenity's skin burned at Taj apparently knowing everything. She knew it shouldn't matter why Ace decided to finally come clean, but she couldn't help but wonder. It wasn't lost on her that the fact that Taj learned about all of this from someone other than her was probably the nail in the coffin of their relationship.

She shook her head, finally letting the tears fall. "I'm so sorry."

"It happened twice, Serenity." Taj's frown started to make way to sadness, which only wrenched her chest more. He took a step towards her but stopped himself. "*Twice.* Do you have any idea what it did to me to hear Ace tell me that you shared yourself with him like that? Hell, that you two were in a serious relationship in the past was enough of a shock..."

"Taj, I know it probably won't mean much to you but I feel so, *so* awful for hurting you," Serenity expressed, her hands clutching the front her shirt. She ached to go over to him, feeling like they hadn't touched in so long. "I should've told you about my past with Ace. I didn't even realize that I was still holding onto any resentment from my time with him, but that's no excuse and I know it. You are everything to me and I've literally been sick since I betrayed you. I've hardly been able to look at myself."

Taj's eyes roamed over her, and he did notice that she'd lost some weight and her skin wasn't as glowing and supple as it usually was; it actually looked dry and there were a couple of healed scratches on her face and neck that had him mildly curious. Dark circles were under her eyes, a testament to her lack of sleep. Her hair was hidden under a colorful head wrap, which he knew she only wore when she thought her hair was looking like crap. He guessed she'd been too wrecked with guilt to pretty up.

"So I guess this explains why you haven't been able to touch me all these months," he surmised in a flat voice.

"Yeah." She sniffed. "I wanted to, but I always got a flashback to what I did. And I knew I should've confessed everything way before now, but I...I was so afraid of losing you."

"How long did you think you could keep this big of a secret, Serenity? This has been hanging over our heads for months; the guilt eating you alive and me thinking I was in a relationship that I wasn't really in. I never would've thought you would do this to me; to *us*. Not in a million years."

"I'm totally in the wrong, Taj. And after hearing that I was mistaken about what I thought I heard that night, I feel even more ridiculous." Hesitating slightly, she eased around the desk and stood in front of him, venturing a brief touch of her hand to his chest before making herself withdraw it, not wanting to push her luck. "And I deserve whatever comes of this. But whether it matters to you or not, I still love you with my whole heart. And I know it's unreasonable and probably even offensive to even say this, but...please forgive me, Taj."

He scoffed. "I'd be more willing to forgive if you'd come clean about all of this on your own. But I found out everything from Ace. If I hadn't come here today, there's no telling *when* we'd finally get everything out on the table. What kind of relationship do we have if we can't even talk to each other? If you're not woman enough to admit when you mess up? You let all this drag out for over a year, Serenity."

She hung her head.

"And even when you thought I betrayed you, you *still* didn't deal with it; you ran yet again. I need to be with someone I can trust, Serenity; somebody who is going to respect me enough to be honest and deal with things head-on. You've shown that's clearly not you. This...I can't do this anymore, Serenity. As much as I love you, the trust is gone and that's..." His voice caught as the emotion of the moment hit him. He briefly turned away, running a hand down his face as he tried to push out the words that caused a searing pain in his chest despite how necessary they were. "It's over."

Hearing those words made Serenity want to crumble to the floor where she stood. It was like she could hear her heart breaking, knowing she and Taj were over. And she only had herself to blame.

Blindly groping for the edge of her desk, she just stood there and cried, the realization of what was happening hitting her full force. She wanted to beg and plead with Taj to give her another chance, but she couldn't find the words. And even if she could, she knew it would be futile. She had betrayed him, twice, with one of his best friends, and kept it from him. All the while letting him pleasure her while she gave him none in return, and with no explanation. There wasn't anything she could say to fix that, and she knew it.

Taj fought to keep his emotions in check as he stood and watched the woman he loved cry her eyes out in front of him. He hated that part of him wanted to take her into his arms and comfort her, despite everything she did. His being angry at her didn't wipe out the love he still had, and the finality of the conversation was starting to make his own legs feel weakened. This was the woman he'd planned to marry. But he didn't know how he could get past everything that had happened.

"I guess we'll have to figure out what to do about the house and stuff," he finally made himself say, his voice a mere grumble. "For the time being, we'll just...keep our distance when we're both there."

Even though that was what they'd essentially been doing for weeks already, knowing that it was now just a kickoff to them separating for good filled Serenity with more pain than she'd ever felt.

"Okay," she whispered, her eyes on the laminate floor.

Figuring there was nothing more to be said, Taj turned to leave. When his hand was on the doorknob, she called out to him.

"What?" he grunted, his back still to her.

"I really do love you. And only you."

"Yeah, I love you, too." He looked at her over his shoulder, his own eyes glistening. "All the more reason that I hate you for doing this to us."

He made himself leave as she buried her face in her hands.

Taj felt like he was in a fog. Ever since he left the café, he'd just driven around in a daze, going nowhere in particular. He knew ending things with Serenity was the right thing to do, but that didn't mean he enjoyed doing it. He'd loved her for over three years and as much as he might've wanted it to, that didn't stop just because she royally messed up.

His phone rang and he didn't even glance at his display to see who it was, thinking it might be Serenity. But when it rang again and he noticed it was Rasheed, he quickly wiped his eyes and sat up straighter, as if his friend could see him, before answering.

"Yeah."

"Hey, man," Rasheed's voice filled the car. "I just wanted to check on you."

"I'm here, that's all I can say."

"Where are you?"

"In the car. Just driving. I, um...I just left the café. Finally confronted Serenity about everything."

"Oh." Rasheed paused. "I take it things didn't go well, huh?"

"No." Taj cleared his throat. "It's over. I ended it."

"Aww damn. I'm so sorry to hear that, man."

"I didn't have a choice."

"I get it. Look...you don't need to be out roaming by yourself right now. Come through."

"How come you're not at work?"

"I'm off already. Worked the early shift."

"Rasheed, I appreciate it, man, but I wouldn't be good company at all right now. I'm still trying to process what just happened."

"And I respect that but you're my boy and I'm worried about you. And there's something I want to talk to you about, anyway."

"What, did you have a turn with Serenity, too? Just tell me now, if you did."

"No, man. That's not it. Can you please just come by here?"

Taj didn't feel like company, but he also wasn't in a hurry to go back to the house he still had to share with Serenity for the time being. And he certainly didn't need to keep driving around wasting gas.

"All right," he conceded. "I'll head that way."

"Thank you."

Since Taj had wandered way to the other side of Terston, it took him a little longer to get to Rasheed's thanks to the afternoon traffic. He rode most of the way in silence, since every station he turned it on seemed to play or say something that reminded him of Serenity.

"I thought you might've changed your mind or something," Rasheed greeted him when he finally arrived. The friends shared a brief hug.

"Traffic." Taj ran a hand over his disheveled short locs and glanced around the sparse living room. "You got anything to eat?"

"I was about to order some pizza. What kind you want?"

"Meat lovers."

Rasheed chose not to comment; he just pulled out his phone and went about placing the order. Taj wasn't a strict vegetarian but he didn't eat a lot of meat, most of the time. Even when he made the cheesesteaks he loved so much, he usually used a meat alternative. The fact that he wanted to gorge on real pepperoni and sausage and ham and whatever else showed how down in the dumps he must have been.

"So what was it you wanted to talk to me about?" Taj asked, plopping onto the couch. "Even though I don't know if I can take any more bad news."

"It's not really *bad* news, but I do feel like I owe you an apology."

"An apology for what?"

"For my part in the whole Ace-and-Serenity thing, as far as knowing about it. I had no clue about the recent time, but I *did* know about what went down last year, even though I wished I didn't."

"Oh." Taj released a long sigh and Rasheed couldn't tell if he was trying to keep any rising anger in check or if he was just processing. "Just out of curiosity, how did you find out?"

"I happened to Facetime Ace and Serenity walked out...undressed."

Taj's face tightened.

"I was hoping maybe it was innocent and she was just taking a shower or something and didn't know he'd be in the room, but they were both looking too caught for that to be it. Ace finally admitted everything when they got back. Of course I had to drag it out of him."

"Umph."

"I told both of them they needed to come clean but they kept punking out. I hated knowing about what went down when you didn't."

"Yeah."

"So...I'm sorry for being a part of keeping you in the dark. I was tempted to tell you myself a few times but figured it needed to come from them."

"You're right, it did. I appreciate your apology, man, but you didn't do anything wrong. I get where you're coming from and all but at the end of the day, they're the ones who betrayed me, not you."

"Yeah." Relieved to have finally gotten that off his chest, Rasheed relaxed against the back of the couch. He eyed his sulking friend. "I'll tell you something else, too."

Taj glanced over at him. "What?"

"I know it might be a wild thing to say now, given where you and Serenity are, but I've always admired your relationship."

Scoffing, Taj rolled his eyes. "I don't know why. Even before all this mess, we were far from perfect, despite how we tried to act like we were."

"Come on, man, *no* relationship is perfect. It wasn't about that. You two chose each other. You had the balls to put your heart out there with no guarantee how it would end up. Not everybody can do that."

"Yeah, well. You see what good it did."

"Even if it didn't end like you wanted it to, once you come down off of being pissed off and hurt and shit, you'll still have a lot of good times with her to think about. They might not matter right now but they will at some point. I'm willing to bet just about anything on that."

Taj looked over at him. Rasheed was tapping his fist on the arm of the couch, his expression thoughtful.

"Is this about you and Iman?"

Shaking his head, Rasheed let his fist drop into his lap. "There is no me and Iman."

"What do you mean?"

"Nothing is happening there, man. Every time I think we might be on the same page..." Rasheed shook his head wearily. "I'm not trying to have a lifelong fuck buddy and that's it."

"Has she said that's all she wants with you?"

"No..."

"Rasheed, man, then why don't you just talk to her and see what it is she wants? You've been dancing around your feelings for her for a while now. Even at couple's night, you both were clearly avoiding saying things flat-out. Neither of you usually have any problem speaking your minds. What's the problem?"

"I don't know what it is, Taj. It's wild, how I lose my head around her. Every time I start to bring it up, I hear her voice in my head telling me she doesn't want what I want. I'm not trying to get my face cracked for nothing."

"Unless you're clairvoyant, you have no way of knowing what she'll say. For all you know, she could want you as much as you want her, and not just for the casual stuff y'all have been doing. Sometimes, 'Sheed, you've just gotta put yourself out there, even if it doesn't turn out like you want. At least then you won't be left forever wondering." Taj nudged Rasheed's shoulder with his fist. "And regardless, there'll still be good times with her for you to think about, right?"

Unable to help his smirk from growing, Rasheed cut his eyes at his friend. "Smart ass."

Just then, both of their phones chimed. Taj was in no hurry to check his, but Rasheed immediately pulled his phone from his pocket. When he read the new text message, he groaned and cursed under his breath.

"What?" Taj asked, grabbing his own phone. When he read the text in their group chat, he sighed and dropped his head.

The message was from Ricky, letting them know he officially moved out.

Chapter 16

Lavinia & Ricky

Lavinia wasn't even sure what day it was. She'd been curled up in bed ever since Ricky piled all of his suitcases into his Tahoe and drove off after telling her he wanted a divorce.

A *divorce*.

There hadn't been anything she could say or do to keep him from leaving. She'd cried, promised whatever she could think of, offered up every sexual favor in the book, but none of it made any difference. His mind was made up, he said. All the time he'd been gone, Lavinia had been so sure that it would only make him realize how much he loved her. But it seemed to just cement how much happier he'd been without her.

"Ricky," she had pleaded, following him down the stairs as he hauled another one of his suitcases to his truck. "Are you serious??"

"What does it look like, Lavinia?"

"How can you just leave like this? Like it's nothing?"

"Because I'm tired of living like this. I'm sick of being unhappy with you."

"What about what we promised, though? When we got married, we said we'd always work through whatever came up together. Did you forget about that??"

"No." Ricky shoved the suitcase into his backseat and slammed the door shut, finally looking at her. "But can you honestly say that you haven't used that as an excuse to yourself to do whatever you wanted, because you thought I wouldn't go anywhere?"

Her mouth opened to deny that, but nothing came out. If she was honest, she knew she *had* thought that very thing; that Ricky might get pissed at her but wouldn't go anywhere at the end of the day, thanks to that promise. Her mother's words about taking advantage of Ricky rang through her head.

"I...maybe I did," she made herself say.

"Maybe, huh?" Ricky shook his head and started to walk past her back into the house.

"Okay, fine! Yes, I did!" she exclaimed, stopping him. "Ricky, I get that I'm not the best wife but am I really *that* terrible that you have to get away from me like this? You're that willing to just throw away all of our years together just because we've hit a rough patch?"

"And I see you still don't listen because if you did, you'd know we've had this conversation already. This is more than just a damn rough patch, Lavinia. This is years of bulldozing and selfishness and frustration all snowballing into this excuse for a marriage we have now. You want everything to be about you; well, now you've got it. You can do whatever you want, which should be easy for you."

"Ricky!" She trailed him back into the house, barely feeling the pebbles she was stepping on with her bare feet. "Just tell me what I need to do; whatever you say, I'll do it. Just please don't leave!"

Stopping abruptly, Ricky turned to look at her. Lavinia looked up at him hopefully, prepared to agree to whatever he was about to demand of her.

"The day I left, I had every intention of trying to work things out with you," he informed her, unmoved by her tears. "I was going to swallow my pride and make the first move to try to get us back on track. Then I went upstairs and overheard you having a conversation with your mother."

Her eyes widened in panic and he could almost see the color drain from her face.

"Apparently I'm just some angry monster who's jealous of you and your career, and apparently that jealousy is affecting my performance in the bedroom since apparently, I haven't been pleasing you there." Ricky folded his arms. "Of course, I'm still able to cheat on you, though, which I'm also apparently doing. And all the while you're just the good, patient little wife who is willing to hold my hand through all of my 'issues', which is why you're so tolerant of my going to see a therapist. Did I forget anything?"

Lavinia felt her entire body go cold. She had no idea he'd heard her say those things.

"What are you being so quiet now for?" Ricky persisted, leaning towards her. "You had plenty to say to your mama when you were spouting all that bullshit, trying to make yourself seem like the victim."

"I'm sorry-"

"The hell you're sorry. You would never have admitted to any of that if I hadn't called you on it."

"I was...I was just talking, baby; it didn't mean anything!"

"Save it. For that bullshit to even come out of your mouth because you thought you could get away with it just shows how little respect you have for me. And I refuse to be with a woman like that."

She lunged for his arm when he started to turn away. "Ricky!"

He yanked himself free. "Don't touch me, Lavinia."

"I said I was sorry!"

"And I said I didn't believe you."

"I don't want you to leave!"

"Oh, well." He grabbed the last of his bags from the bed and looked around the room to make sure he didn't leave anything. "It's happening, and you can thank yourself for it. I'm sure you'll conjure up some other bullshit to tell your mama or your girls to absolve yourself of any responsibility for all this, but at this point, I don't even give a fuck. You'll be getting the divorce papers soon enough."

Feeling her stomach drop to her feet, Lavinia reached out and grabbed the bedpost to steady herself. "Divorce?"

"Yes, divorce. There's no need in dragging this out." He stalked towards the door as she stood frozen in place, too shocked to move. "And I'll be changing my number but in the meantime, quit calling me. We don't have anything else to say to each other."

The front door slammed loudly several moments later, snapping Lavinia out of her momentary trance. She rushed over to the window just in time to see Ricky's Tahoe speed down the street, away from her.

Now, she didn't know what to do with herself. Whatever anger she'd managed to conjure up towards Ricky for leaving fizzled out as soon as she managed to get it ignited. As stubborn as she usually was, she had to glumly admit that she had driven her husband out the door. And there didn't seem to be anything she could do about it.

She reached for her phone, wishing there was some kind of message from Ricky, even if it was an angry one. But of course, nothing. There were missed calls and texts from her mother, father, Iman, and Charmaine. Suddenly, she felt the urge to be around her girls, including Serenity. Lavinia hadn't had much to say to her ever since the night Serenity confessed to cheating on Taj with Ace, but at the moment, that didn't matter. It wasn't like Lavinia had any kind of high horse to sit on.

She sent a message to their group chat, asking them to come over, and was relieved to get almost immediate responses letting her know they'd be by as soon as they could. Serenity didn't respond, and Lavinia tried to contact her separately and plead to get her to agree to come, but got no answer. By the time Lavinia dragged herself out of bed, took a shower, and threw on some leggings and a t-shirt, her doorbell was ringing.

"Hey, what's going on?" Charmaine asked, stepping forward to give her a much-needed hug. "I got here as soon as I could."

"Thank you for coming, girl," Lavinia droned.

"Of course. I think Iman is right behind me."

"Good. And just so you know, I asked Serenity to come, too."

Charmaine stilled. "Please don't tell me this is some kind of intervention because I'm still not-"

"It's not an intervention. I just need all the support I can get right now so I hope you two can be in the same room with each other. That's if she even shows up; she hasn't responded to my message."

"Hmph." Charmaine went further into the living room, removing her jacket. "Since this is about whatever you're dealing with, I'll behave."

"Thank you. Because I don't have the energy to pull you off of her right now."

Shortly afterwards, Iman arrived, with Serenity showing up right behind her. The tension was clearly evident between her and Charmaine, but as promised, Charmaine didn't cause a scene, though she barely acknowledged Serenity.

"Thank y'all for coming by," Lavinia told them once they were all congregated in the living room. "I just needed to be around my people right now."

"What happened?" Iman asked her.

Lavinia looked down at her hands, feeling the ball sprout up in her throat at the answer she wished she didn't have to give. "Ricky left. For good, this time. He moved out. Right after announcing he was divorcing me."

Gasps went up around her.

"When?" Iman asked, placing a hand on her shoulder.

"A couple of days ago. When I got home from work and saw his truck here, I got all excited, thinking he was ready to start working things out. But he was just here packing his things."

"Wow, I have to admit that I thought he just needed some time to himself; I didn't expect him to actually move out," Charmaine commented.

"You and me both. It totally threw me."

"Did y'all have another fight or something?"

"No. We hadn't even talked while he'd been staying in the hotel or wherever he was. But I'll be real and admit that it was my mouth that ran him out the door."

The ladies glanced at each other, no one wanting to admit that they weren't surprised to hear that.

"What did you say?" Iman finally asked.

Lavinia ran down the things she'd told her mother when she didn't know Ricky had been listening, and they all winced in response.

"Lavinia, you didn't," Charmaine groaned, sinking in her seat.

"Damn, girl," Iman added, shaking her head.

Serenity remained quiet, not feeling like she deserved to condemn her friend, though her slightly-sunken eyes spoke volumes.

"I didn't know he was listening!" Lavinia defended.

"You shouldn't have said that stuff in the first place," Iman retorted. "You know good and well that was some bullshit. And Ricky didn't deserve that."

"I know he didn't." Lavinia sighed. "But I guess it's easier to blame him for eavesdropping than admit that I shouldn't have been saying all that. Which is apparently part of his problem with me, the fact that I can never admit when I'm wrong."

"Do you see where he's coming from with that?" Charmaine asked. "Because I love you, but he's got a point. That's not exactly your strong suit."

"Can't say it's the first time I've heard it."

"If you know that, then why haven't you done something about it?"

Part of Lavinia regretted inviting her friends over; she didn't appreciate getting scolded like this. But the voice in her head told her to check herself. It was her own fault that she was in this position and she couldn't be mad at anyone for pointing that out, as hard as it was to hear.

"I can admit that I didn't really believe he'd go anywhere, regardless of what I did," she admitted. Blowing out a long breath, her eyes flitted up to the wooden beams on the ceiling. "I took him for granted, took advantage of him, all that. I get it. And now I'm paying the price for it."

"And you don't think there's any way he'll reconsider and come back?"

"Short of me winding up pregnant, I doubt there's anything I could say to get him back in this house. And seeing as how we haven't had sex since couple's night, I can't even hope for that."

"That damn couple's night," Iman muttered, shaking her head. "A whole lot of shit surely changed after that."

"Boy, did it," Charmaine concurred. "But, honestly, unearthing all of that stuff was necessary. Clearly we all had things we needed to get off our chests that we probably wouldn't have on our own. And there's no way to fix things if you don't know what's wrong."

"I guess." Lavinia looked over at Serenity, who had yet to say a word. She just sat curled up in the armchair alone even though there was plenty of room on the couch where the three of them were. Lavinia recalled how she'd bought the couch despite how much Ricky hated it, and another wave of shame washed over her. "Serenity, how are you doing?"

Her eyes widening in surprise, Serenity gave a halfhearted shrug. "We don't have to talk about me. I'm only here because you asked me to come."

"Right, I asked you to come, which means I wanted you to be here. You don't have to shrink away in the corner."

"I know you all are still upset at me and I don't blame you. We don't have to pretend otherwise."

"Serenity." Lavinia sat forward, looking at her weary friend with concern. Serenity looked worse than she'd ever seen her. Her face was breaking out, she looked like she hadn't slept in days, and her clothes were hanging off of her. Lavinia could tell when they hugged at the door that her friend's usually lush body wasn't what it used to be. "Girl, I can't speak for anybody else, but I'm not even thinking about all that. Clearly, I am in *no* position to look down my nose at you. At the end of the day, regardless of how we got here, we're essentially in the same boat. Let's just be here for each other."

Her chin quivering, Serenity's hand went to her haphazard head wrap, then to her cheek, then to her chest. She swallowed, pulling her bottom lip between her teeth as she fought what felt like the millionth round of tears she'd shed over the past couple of days.

"Taj ended things," she finally admitted, suddenly sounding hoarse. She cleared her throat as her fingers mindlessly ran back and forth along her thigh. "He confronted me, we had it out, and...that was it."

"Serenity, girl, I'm sorry," Iman sighed, moving over to sit on the arm of the chair and slide an arm around her friend. She pulled her closer, rubbing her shoulder with the warmth and comfort Serenity clearly needed. "I really am. Regardless of what you did, I know you love Taj."

"I do. I really do." Serenity sniffed, her eyes on her sliding hand as her head leaned against Iman. "But I brought it on myself. I made one amazingly stupid decision after another and...I can't blame him for leaving me. As much as it hurts, I'll just have to learn to live with it."

"I know you're trying to be strong right now and I respect that, but it's okay to be vulnerable around us. Believe me, you're not the only one that has messed up."

Iman shot a pointed look at Charmaine, who pursed her lips and looked away defiantly. Charmaine had been fully prepared to pretend like Serenity wasn't even there, but try as she might, she couldn't make herself not care at all about what she was going through. The constant reminder of her own indiscretion with Tango kept a reign on any judgmental rants she was tempted to launch.

"I'm fine," Serenity insisted, convincing no one. "We, um, we don't have to talk about me anymore. I'm getting what I deserved. We're supposed to be here for Lavinia."

After another searing glare from Iman, Charmaine finally sighed and sat forward in her seat. "Serenity."

Serenity's hand stilled as she turned hesitant eyes towards Charmaine.

"Me and you...we still have some issues to work out and I know that. But even though I might not be over what you did, that doesn't mean I'm enjoying seeing you like this. We're all dealing with heavy stuff right now and like Lavinia said, we should just be here for each other and put everything else on pause for the time being. I'm willing to do that if you are."

Her trembling lips stretching into a grateful smile, Serenity nodded so hard her head wrap wobbled. "I'd love that."

Iman grabbed Serenity's hand and pulled her over to the couch with Charmaine and Lavinia, and the four friends spent the rest of the evening confessing, venting, and encouraging each other. All of their problems might not have been fixed by the time they finally dispersed, but they at least knew they had each other to lean on as they dealt with them.

Chapter 17

Iman & Rasheed

Rasheed knew it was past time for him to man up and finally have the conversation he'd been avoiding with Iman.

Taj's advice had been heavy on his mind, not to mention everything he'd heard from Ricky and Ace about growing some balls and just coming clean with Iman about how he felt about her. Rasheed had never thought of himself as a punk, but this new level of feelings had him frustratingly gun-shy. Even if Iman didn't respond like he hoped he would, he knew he needed to go ahead and find out what the deal was with them either way.

He invited her over, and his nerves began tingling as soon as she (hesitantly) agreed. Feeling the need to do something special, he rushed to the store thirty minutes before she was to arrive and bought flowers, balloons, and some chocolates and honeybuns. He raced back to his place and arranged his hasty purchases around his bedroom, then thought better of it and moved everything to the living room. He didn't want her to think it was a booty call.

By the time Iman was knocking on the door, Rasheed had only marginally calmed down. He told himself to get it together as he went to answer the door.

"Hey, Rasheed," Iman greeted him, a hint of shyness in her brown eyes.

"Hey. Uh, come in."

Stepping inside, he pulled her in for a hug, burying his face in the crook of her neck. She smelled amazing, as usual. And he felt encouraged at how hard she was squeezing him back.

"You changed your hair," he observed once they finally parted.

"Oh, yeah." Iman snaked her long nails through her shoulder-length hair, having removed her black and grey braids during her day of beauty with Charmaine the day before. Her tresses were now a deep auburn color and Rasheed's jaw clenched at how amazing it looked on her. "Figured it was time to switch it up. You like it?"

"Hell yeah. It's hot."

Grinning, she reached up and stroked his beard. "I appreciate that."

It was then that she noticed the flowers and balloons and treats that were strewn along the coffee table and couch. She glanced around the room curiously before turning her eyes back to Rasheed.

"Are you expecting somebody else after me?"

"What? No!"

"Then what's up with all this? It's not even close to Valentine's Day and even if it was, I've never known you to do this kind of stuff."

Rasheed made himself fight the feeling of ridiculousness that was starting to creep over him. "I guess I felt the need to switch it up, too. Iman...there's a reason I called you over here."

She straightened slightly, her expression flattening. "What is it?"

Motioning for her to sit down, Rasheed slid the candy and honeybuns on the couch to one side before joining her on the other. "This is something I should've told you a while ago, when it first started hitting me. But I admit I kept talking myself out of it."

Tensing, Iman folded her arms across her waist, clutching her elbows. Her eyes drifted from his face. "I'm listening."

"I know we said we'd just keep things light and casual between us, but I'm not with that anymore, Iman. At some point, my feelings changed. I'm...I'm into you. Like, *really* into you. If I'm being all the way real about it, I've fallen for you. And I just need to know what you think about that because I can't keep going on like we have been. I can't just be friends with benefits anymore."

Several moments passed with Iman just staring at him, and part of him regretted what he said, even though he'd meant every word. Then he wondered if maybe he just said it the wrong way, though he couldn't tell if she was upset or not. She was just staring at him.

"Iman?"

Snapping out of it, Iman finally cleared her throat, her false lashes fluttering rapidly. "Oh wow...you kinda threw me for a loop with that, Rasheed."

"I get that. But I had to let you know."

"I'm glad you did." Her hand grabbed his. "Because I'm feel the same way."

Now stumped himself, Rasheed's eyebrows shot to his hairline. "Are you serious?"

"Dead ass. I wouldn't joke about that. Especially since I've been trying to work up the nerve to tell you the same thing."

He blinked, shocked. "I've never known you to be bashful."

"I could say the same about you. But I guess it's a whole different thing when these kinds of feelings get involved. Nobody wants to get hurt."

"The last thing I wanna do is hurt you, Iman," Rasheed insisted, his fingers tightening around hers. "I want this thing between us to be real, not just a fling. I'm over this fuck buddy shit."

"You and me both; you have no idea." Iman glanced around them. "So is that why you got all this stuff?"

"Yeah," Rasheed admitted, feeling his face flush. "Though it seems stupid now. Like I'm in fifth grade or some shit."

Iman giggled, sliding closer to him and lifting a leg over his. "No, it's not stupid. I appreciate that you wanted to do it. Though I hope you know that's not what I need from you."

"It isn't?"

"This stuff isn't you, Rasheed." Iman waved a hand at the balloons and flowers. "You're romantic in your own way; like how you make sure to have something to eat for me when I come over after work, or when you send me things you know will make me laugh when I'm having a bad day, or when you rub my back until I fall asleep. I love that. You don't ever have to be anything but yourself around me."

Tired of resisting, Rasheed leaned forward and pressed his lips to hers, palming the side of her face. The relief of hearing that she wanted the kind of relationship he wanted was almost overwhelming, and he wanted to kick himself for waiting so long to admit it.

Iman matched the intensity of his kiss, her hands gripping his shirt to keep him close. She hadn't known what to expect when he asked her to come over and had prepared herself to hear that they were done. It was a shock when he told her that his feelings matched hers. She could just imagine the teasing her girls would give her when they found out.

But she wasn't going to worry about that now. For the time being, she just wanted to savor the moment with her man. Finally thinking of Rasheed in that way sent a jolt of giddiness through her that she hadn't felt in years, if ever.

Pulling her onto his lap, Rasheed wrapped his arms tightly around Iman, needing to be closer to her. Her arms encircled his neck as she deepened the kiss, neither of them in a hurry for it to end.

"Hey," she whispered when they finally tapered off. She rested her forehead to his.

His hands slid tenderly up and down her back. "Hey."

"I love you, Rasheed."

Emotion at her words warmed him, and his fingers gripped her so hard that she actually gasped. "I love you, too."

"So we're official, right? We're claiming each other and everything?"

"Make it known, baby. We're as official as it gets. This is locked in."

She grinned. "So I guess you'd better let that touchy-feely chick from your job know that she'd better keep her hands to herself 'cause you've got a woman now that does not like other women messing with what's hers. She needs to find somebody else to flirt with."

"I'll be sure to let her know. And same goes for any dudes that have been sniffing up behind you. Your man doesn't like that shit. You are *mine*, Iman."

"Trust me, you don't have anything to worry about, baby." She snaked her nails through his hair, unable to resist grinning at hearing him claim her like that. She was already hooked on it. "You're the only man I want. It's just you and me. And I'm all in."

"Same." He pressed a kiss to the base of her neck.

"And can we make a promise right now to always be honest with each other, even when it's difficult?" Her eyes slid closed as Rasheed's lips slid further up her neck. "I'm know stuff isn't always gonna be all rosy but I don't wanna go through what our friends are going through right now."

"Trust, I don't, either. Let's do our best to use them as an example of what *not* to do. Even though we were both some punks about admitting our feelings until now."

"True. But now we know. Let's just agree not to make that mistake again and keep it moving. Together."

"No arguments here."

Reclaiming her lips, Rasheed lifted her just enough so he could swivel her onto her back on top of the candy and honeybuns on the couch, her legs clamping around his waist as she held his face in her hands. All thoughts of their friends and anything else were forgotten as they consummated their new relationship, not leaving each other's side for the rest of the night.

Chapter 18

Charmaine & Ace

Ace and Charmaine had been out to dinner countless times over the course of their relationship, but they were each nervous as they headed to Black 47, one of their favorite restaurants. Charmaine usually got excited about their desserts that came courtesy of her favorite pastry chef Camilla Holliday, but all she could think about was how this evening was going to end up.

Things between them had been as okay as could be expected since they'd agreed to try to work things out after everything that had happened, but there was still a thin line of precariousness hanging between them. Ace often felt as if he was walking on eggshells, fearing saying or doing something that would remind Charmaine of his mistakes and set her off. And Charmaine had been doing her best to stop being such a nag and start appreciating Ace for the reasons that made her fall for him in the first place; his sense of humor, his affection, his determination to take care of her. Ace might not have been perfect, but neither was she.

"You look amazing, babe," Ace complimented once they were seated at their table. His eyes roamed over her appreciatively. "I still can't believe you cut your hair but I love it. It really makes your eyes pop."

Charmaine ran a hand down the back of her new short, tapered haircut. She had admittedly freaked out a little when she was in the stylist's chair and the first clump of her hair hit the floor, but it was steadily growing on her. With the cut, the slightly darker brown color, and the matte red lipstick Iman had helped her pick out, she couldn't help but feel sexier than she'd ever felt. She'd been sneaking looks in the mirror ever since the day she returned from the salon.

"I appreciate it, Ace," she replied with a smile. "You're looking mighty handsome, yourself."

"Really?" He eyed her as if he thought she was joking.

It was then that Charmaine realized she didn't compliment Ace as much as she used to. She didn't even realize when she had gotten away from that.

"Yes, really," she assured him, sliding her hand over his. "Very handsome. Thanks for bringing me out tonight."

His hand turning under hers, he stroked the soft underside of her wrist. "I know we haven't been out in a while. Even before everything blew up, I tried to remember the last time we went on a date and couldn't."

"Sounds like we both got too complacent."

"We did. I know *I* did. But I'm gonna fix that."

Charmaine smiled at him, amazed at the changes she'd seen in him in the days since their reconciliation. He was still the same Ace, but more mature and mindful of what came out of his mouth. It gave her hope that they really could go the distance together, since they were both so willing to work on themselves for the betterment of their relationship.

And Ace had been surprisingly cooperative in counseling. They'd only gone to a couple of sessions so far, but he wasn't holding anything back like she feared he would. He was taking it seriously, and so was she.

It helped that they both loved Dr. Claire Burns, who was counseling them. She had even shared some things she'd gone through with her husband, Montrel. Charmaine and Ace had been shocked that not only would she share such personal things with them, but that she was so happy in her marriage after what she described, which they were sure wasn't the extent of it. Them winding up together and happy after all that gave Chamaine and Ace hope for their own relationship.

The waitress brought their drinks and took their orders, and once she was gone, Ace turned his focus back to Charmaine.

"So about the waffle restaurant..."

Automatically tensing, Charmaine fought the automatic frown from peppering her expression. "Yeah?"

"I'm scrapping it."

She exhaled a loud sigh of relief before she could stop herself, and Ace chuckled. "Please tell me you're not teasing me, Ace."

"No, I'm serious. I thought about everything you've been saying all this time that I've been too stubborn to listen to; you were right about it being too big a risk. And opening a restaurant when I have no experience in that industry just because I want to compete with an old classmate is just...stupid."

Charmaine was glad he was the one to say it. "I'm so glad to hear you say that, sweetie, you have *no* idea."

"I still want to have my own thing, but I'll choose something that's better suited for me. Maybe we can even go into something together."

"Yeah, maybe. It would be cool for us to start a business together at some point. But we don't have to rush into that. I mainly want to focus on making sure our relationship is back on track, first and foremost."

"Oh, most definitely," he assured. "Our relationship will always be priority number one, babe. I'm not trying to do anything else to mess this up."

She gazed at him for a moment before reaching over and reclaiming his hand. "Ace, I appreciate all of this effort you're making. But please know I still want you to be yourself. We're both gonna make mistakes; I don't want you to focus so hard on trying not to mess up that you forget to just be my Ace."

"Thanks, for saying that." He hesitated. "You know there's still the subject we've both been dancing around."

"Yeah." Charmaine took a sip of her wine. "It's still a little of a sore subject but...Serenity and I are inching towards getting some semblance of our friendship back. It still hurts some when I think of what happened between you two..."

Ace winced.

"But then I remind myself that I did my dirt, too," she continued. "And if I'm gonna forgive you and try to move past it, I need to try to do the same with her, too. As wrong as she was, I know she's not an inherently malicious person. Plus, she's been going *through* it since her and Taj broke up. He told her she could stay in the house until she found somewhere else to stay, but she couldn't stand being there with him basically treating her like a stranger. She went to stay with Lavinia. I just can't make myself turn my back on her, as much as the petty part of me still wants to."

"I still hate that I had a hand in them splitting up," Ace said, his voice pained. He sat back in his chair. "As thrilled as I am that you and I are trying to work it out, I hate that Taj and Serenity couldn't do the same. I know he loved the hell outta her."

"Honestly, I thought Taj would have reconsidered by now," Charmaine admitted. "But I guess he couldn't get past it."

"He hasn't had any words for me, either. I tried to give him some time, hoping we could finally talk it out but he blocked me. Guess he meant it when he said I was dead to him."

Charmaine felt for Ace. Even though he had absolutely been in the wrong for what he did with Serenity, she felt for him because she knew he was hurting over his ruined friendship with Taj.

"I'm sorry, sweetie."

He shook his head. "It's my own fault. I broke the code; I deserve it."

"I still have to believe that Taj will get to the point where he'll at least be willing to get on speaking terms with you again, even if you might not get back to where you were, friendship-wise. He's always been the most reasonable one out of all of us. I don't think it's in his heart for him to truly hate anyone."

"Even if he doesn't hate me, it doesn't mean he'll want to deal with me again." Ace shook his head, forcing himself to sit up straighter. "But that's not something I have any control over so I just have to...leave it up to him, I guess. I'm here when and if he's ready to talk."

The waitress arrived with their food a few moments later, and their conversation stilled as they enjoyed their meals. Ace was trying to put the idea of Taj never forgiving him out of his mind, and Charmaine was trying to block out the residual images of Ace and Serenity flashing through hers. They were coming less and less, and she could only hope that they'd disappear altogether in time.

After they'd enjoyed their steak dinners and desserts of goat cheese cheesecake with roasted figs for Charmaine and chocolate turtle layer cake for Ace, they headed home. They each had a lot on their minds so they weren't saying much, but the silence wasn't strained. Charmaine's hand rested on Ace's thigh as he drove, and he'd lift it to his lips whenever he came to a red light.

There was still a certain awkwardness that hung over them when they were home alone at night, though, and they both felt it as soon as they walked through the door. As they'd been working on their relationship, one area they'd pressed pause on was intimacy. They'd each gotten tested since Ace had admitted to wearing no protection when he slept with Serenity either time (which Charmaine had thoroughly cursed him out for) and they were both in the clear health-wise, but they hadn't shared a bed since they reconciled, each having issues they were still battling as far as getting past each other's physical indiscretions.

But as Ace promised, he'd gotten rid of the incriminating couch in the den. And true to her word, Charmaine hadn't been back to Pure Sugar or had any further contact with Tango.

Ace grabbed some sweats to change into and went to the guest bedroom, choosing to give Charmaine her privacy while she got undressed in their room, even though everything in him wanted to stay in there with her. He was still trying to get to where he didn't think about what she did, but that didn't mean his desire for her was gone. He missed making love to her, but he would've been more than happy with just holding her at night. Sleeping alone down the hall from her wasn't ideal, but he knew it was only temporary. They had each admitted they needed some time and even though he felt he was ready to move past that, he had to respect it if Charmaine wasn't there yet.

He was lying across the full-sized bed, deep in thought with his arm over his eyes, when there was a soft knock on the door. It was so soft he almost missed it, but when he heard it again, he shot up and scurried over to it with a curious frown.

That morphed into spine-freezing shock when he saw his fiancée standing there in a red silk nightie.

Charmaine couldn't help but grin as Ace stood there slack-jawed. His eyes roamed up and down her body and back again, and she could see his hand start to reach for her, but he stopped himself.

Stepping forward, she grabbed his hands and placed them around her waist. "You don't have to hold back anymore, Ace." She captured his thick bottom lip between hers as she slid his hands underneath the short hem of her nightie. "You can touch me. I *want* you to touch me."

Ace groaned as he felt his manhood immediately harden to cement. His hands squeezed the soft skin of her bottom, loving that he was being given this access again. When she touched her tongue to his, he eagerly returned her kiss, backing her against the doorjamb and pressing his body against hers.

Before things got too heated, though, he made himself pull back. Both their chests were heaving with still-unleashed pent-up desire.

"What's wrong?" she panted.

"Are you sure about this, babe?" he felt compelled to ask. His fingertips skimmed along her upper thighs, his jaws clenching as his gaze fell to her cleavage. He hated that he'd ever suggested she change her breasts because they were perfect for him just as they were. "Don't mistake, I *really* want all of you, but Dr. Burns said-"

"Fuck that," Charmaine interjected with a finger to his lips. "This is one area I'm not trying to listen to her on. I'm tired of sleeping down the hall from you, touching myself when I really want your hands on me."

"And you're sure this won't bring up any thoughts about...you know..."

"Only one way to find out, isn't there?" She grabbed his behind and pulled him closer to her, then looked up at him with mild concern. "Unless *you're* worried about having thoughts about...you know."

A tiny part of Ace *was* worried about seeing images of that baking busta Tango kissing and touching on his woman flash through his mind as they made love, but the larger part of him wanted her too much to let that stop anything. At some point, they were going to have to take steps to move past that or else they'd stay stuck where they were, pining away for each other at night in separate bedrooms mere steps from each other.

"Like you said, only one way to find out." He grabbed the back of her head and crashed his lips onto hers, and she immediately began clawing at his shirt. In mere moments, all of their clothes were on the ground and Charmaine was pushing Ace onto the bed, climbing onto him with a naughty grin.

"*I'm* on top this time," she declared, taking his dick in her hand and giving it a few firm strokes. She leaned down and swirled her tongue around the head, loving the shiver that ripped through Ace when she did. "If that's all right with you."

"Anything you want is all right with me," he breathed, his hands gripping the sheets as she slid her warm mouth further over his shaft. Whispered curses fell from his mouth unchecked as she leisurely but eagerly sucked him. He loved how bold she was being and wasn't about to do anything to stop or question it.

And when she finally mounted him and started riding him like she never had, Ace forgot about everything else and reveled in the moment, more thankful than he'd ever been.

He had his Charmaine back.

Chapter 19

Lavinia & Ricky

Lavinia didn't know if it was divine intervention or what, but Ricky had finally agreed to sit down and have a talk with her.

It shocked her speechless when he called and let her know he'd be by the house as soon as he could get off work. She almost hadn't answered because she didn't recognize the number, but then she remembered what he'd said about changing his phone number and hoped it might be him. And finally, one of her prayers was being answered.

"This isn't a joke, is it?" she couldn't resist asking, gripping the phone in her hand as if she was preparing to hear that it was. "Are you messing with me?"

"No," Ricky had replied simply. "You want me to come by or not?"

"Yes! Yes, of course!"

"All right, then. I'll be by later on."

Lavinia was sure that Taj or Rasheed probably had a hand in getting Ricky to hear her out, and she'd have to give them each a big basket of beer or some sports tickets or something in thanks. But for the time being, she had to make sure she didn't put her foot in her mouth and make things worse.

Serenity offered to make herself scarce when she heard about Ricky coming over. Lavinia had loved having her there so they could help each other through this hard time they were both enduring. It had been a big help, not having to go home to an empty house and having someone there she could vent to. Not to mention, even a distraught Serenity still made the best apple pie.

But Lavinia could tell that Serenity felt some kind of way about seeing apparent progress between Lavinia and Ricky when Taj was still shutting her out. Even though Serenity tried to insist that she had accepted that she had blown it with Taj and that they were over, Lavinia knew better. If Taj told her he wanted her back, Serenity would be on the first thing smoking back to their house and they both knew it.

"Where are you gonna go?" Lavinia asked Serenity, who was massaging moisturizer through her short natural hair. She'd finally let go of the head wraps when Lavinia managed to convince her to let her wash and trim it for her, both of which were badly needed. Serenity still looked like walking exhaustion since her nights in bed mostly consisted of tossing and turning, ending in her giving up and utilizing Lavinia's barely-used streaming services until she dozed off an hour or two before she had to be up again, and Lavinia was still worried about her.

"I need to go by the café; I've been leaving everything to my employees, only checking in by phone most of the time. I'll stay there until closing and then probably just go to a movie or something."

"You know it's probably okay if you just hang out in the guest room while Ricky is here. If you keep your door closed, I'm sure he won't care. I trust you not to eavesdrop."

"No, you two should be alone. I wouldn't feel right being here. It's fine, really."

Lavinia eyed her friend as she checked her purse to make sure she wasn't forgetting anything. "I'm still worried about you, girl. I know you're still hurting bad, no matter how hard you try to keep your game face on."

Keeping her face averted, Serenity shrugged. "I'm dealing with it. It would help if you and Iman would stop reminding me of it, though. I know you're concerned and I love you for it, but I'd really appreciate it if y'all would just please stop asking me about Taj or our failed relationship. I'm just trying to accept that it's over and move on, like he is."

Choosing to let it go, Lavina just pursed her lips and nodded, conceding. "I'll try not to mention it again."

"Thank you." Serenity slung her purse over her shoulder and crossed over to Lavinia, giving her a firm hug. "I appreciate you; you've really been here for me."

"Of course. We're like sisters, you know that."

"I know." Serenity flashed a smile that wasn't as bright as the ones she was known for. "Good luck with Ricky. I'll check before I come back to make sure it's okay, or to see if I need to find somewhere else to go."

"Okay. I can't imagine he'll be here that long."

"You never know." Serenity winked at her before brushing past, heading towards the front door and gently closing it behind her.

Once she was alone, Lavinia felt her nerves return as she waited for Ricky. He hadn't given her an exact time when he'd be showing up, so she couldn't do anything but wait. She tried to occupy herself with looking over some things for work, but her head wasn't in it. There wasn't anything she wanted to see on television. She tried to call Iman, but she was with Rasheed;

thankfully they had stopped being stubborn and admitted how they felt about each other, and had been glued to each other's side ever since. And Lavinia already knew that Charmaine was spending the evening with Ace.

Her mother Darla had left her a message, but Lavinia was in no hurry to return it. The irrational part of her brain blamed her mother for egging on the things Ricky had overheard her say that day, even though the rational part of Lavinia knew that the fault was hers. No one had forced her to say any of the nonsense she'd spouted. But it was easier for her to share the blame, even if it was just in her own head.

By the time Ricky finally arrived, Lavinia had dozed off on the couch. He stood over her, looking at her in her fitted white v-neck tee, dark jeans, and bare feet, her long hair extensions falling over her face. There was a tiny part of him that was tempted to leave, but he made himself keep his feet from moving.

He started to reach down and shake her awake, but stopped himself. Instead he barked, "Lavinia."

She jumped, her eyes popping open. She'd always been a relatively light sleeper. Her hand swiped her hair from her face as she sat up. "Hey." She yawned. "When'd you get here?"

"Just now." He took a seat in the armchair. Lavinia noticed that he didn't bother removing his coat. "So, what's up?"

Momentarily stumped, Lavinia just stared at him. "Honestly, I'm not sure, Ricky. I'm a little surprised you're even here. You were pretty adamant about being done with me so hopefully you can understand my being stumped about what to say."

"You were practically begging me to talk to you. Now I'm here and you don't have any words?"

"Ricky..." She could sense he was already aggravated and she had to keep her own frustration in check. "I know I wanted you here, but is there honestly *anything* I could say that would make any difference? Because if you're here to humiliate me or just sit and let me spill my heart out and then walk out again without a word, then let's not. I can't take that."

He glared at her before running a hand down his face and sitting back in his seat with a sigh. He'd made a promise to himself and his therapist (and his friends) that he'd be amicable and he needed to try to stick to that.

"I'm not here to humiliate you," he verified, trying to take the edge out of his voice. His therapist had been working with him on his anger towards his wife, and to his surprise, being in front of her now wasn't the skin-burning experience he expected it to be. "Let's just...say whatever needs to be said."

Telling herself to think positively, Lavinia sat up a little straighter. "All right, well...I know I've said it already, but I'm saying it again; I really am so sorry for all that stuff I said to Mama that day about you."

"That's all you have to apologize for?"

"No...I know I haven't been the easiest wife to live with. I get now how I used what I knew about your past to get what I wanted, even though I wasn't consciously thinking that at the time. It wasn't fair to you. Apparently, I've gotten a little too used to getting my way."

"You realized this on your own?"

Not sure if this was a trick question, Lavinia hesitated. "I mean...Mama pointed it out to me. But I had to stop being stubborn and own up to it. You used to always be so happy and easygoing, Ricky, and now I can't even remember the last time I've seen you smile. Knowing I'm a big part of the reason for that is...well, it's humbling. I love you so much and I hate that I drove you to that."

He eyed her. "You still love me?"

She nodded, knowing she looked more eager than she probably should. Her eyes held his gaze as she replied, "I absolutely do."

They looked at each other for several moments before his eyes shifted to the side wall. Lavinia itched to ask if he still loved her in return, but uncharacteristically, she didn't have the nerve. She didn't think she'd be able to handle it if the answer was no.

"Clearly, I still care about you," Ricky finally spoke up. "Or else I wouldn't bother to be here."

Hope surged through her. "Good to know."

"I noticed you're taking your time signing the divorce papers."

"I took them to my lawyer but...couldn't bring myself to sign them yet."

"Did you think something was going to change?"

"I hoped it would. Prayed it would."

"And how long did you plan on holding out?"

"I don't know." Her hands briefly pressed against her cheeks before dropping back to her lap and disappearing between her ample thighs. "I wasn't scheming; just trying to keep hope alive until I had absolutely no choice not to."

"Hmm." Ricky noted how subdued she was, which wasn't what he was used to. Lavinia had always been loud and self-assured, even when she was wrong. And nine times out of ten, she was way too stubborn to admit *when* she was wrong. He was mildly encouraged at how willing she seemed to humble herself and hoped to high heaven it wasn't a front.

"All right," he said, standing. He slid his coat from his shoulders and draped it across the back of the chair before moving over to sit on the opposite end of the couch from his visibly-surprised wife. "Let's do this, then. Let's get everything out on the table. No holding anything back, no lies, no games, no bullshit. Can you handle that?"

"Yes," Lavinia quickly assured, the nerves already starting to overtake her but she knew this was what they needed. "I can handle that."

So they faced each other on the couch and had it out. Going back years into their marriage, Ricky unleashed everything he had held his tongue about, his anger causing him to raise his voice at times and he had to remind himself to stay calm. A lot of the things he revealed as bothersome or upsetting sincerely surprised Lavinia, and she realized just how long things had been building to where they were now.

Lavinia also got some things off of her chest, although her grievances weren't nearly as extensive or intense as Ricky's. Despite the somewhat shallow nature of some of her complaints, Ricky could hear his therapist's voice in his head reminding him to be respectful and not automatically dismissive just because she said something he found ridiculous.

"It really made me feel some kind of way when you never complimented me, Ricky," she told him, unable to help the testiness in her voice. "I'd put on sexy stuff and you wouldn't even notice."

"So you're trying to tell me that when you wear all that inappropriate shit to work, that was for *my* benefit?"

"For mine *and* for yours. Of course I wanted my husband to be turned on by me. And I wish you would quit saying what I wear to work is inappropriate."

"And I wish you'd quit trying to act like it's not. You can't tell me no one there has *ever* commented on it, or that none of your clients have ever looked at you some kind of way."

She started to deny it, but the voice in her head reminded Lavinia that she had agreed to total honesty.

"Fine, it's come up," she admitted grudgingly.

"With your boss or coworkers?"

"Yes. And with clients."

Ricky frowned. "How has it come up with clients?"

"I've been sexually harassed a few times. Propositioned. As recently as a few days ago. Some men spent more time paying attention to my titties or my ass than anything else."

Even though Ricky had surmised something like that could happen and part of him wasn't surprised, what he wasn't expecting was the anger that coursed through him upon hearing about another man coming onto his wife.

"And what did you do about it?" he asked her. "Did you ever indulge any of them?"

"No. Never. I admit that I...I might have flirted some to help deal the deal, but that's all it was about for me. I've told you about my only slip-up with anybody and that was when Marshawn kissed me at that party. I'm always quick to tell any horny clients that I'm a married woman and nothing is gonna happen with them."

Hearing that left Ricky with unexpected relief. When he looked down, he saw his fists had clenched at some point without him realizing it.

"Good."

His voice had been low, but she still heard him. Her lips twitched into a smile.

When there was finally nothing left to be said and they were both emotionally spent, they just sat there leaning against their respective arms of the couch. Lavinia braced herself for him to get up and leave with no indication of what any of this meant for them, but he didn't.

"Have you eaten?" she finally asked him.

Barely lifting his head, he replied simply, "No."

"I can fix you something."

"All right."

Pushing herself up, Lavinia stretched and headed towards the kitchen. Ricky glanced after her, but stayed where he was, still processing the evening. To his surprise, he wasn't that anxious to leave. He wasn't delusional enough to think that all of their issues had been fixed by one conversation, but he believed that Lavinia finally understood where he was coming from, and recognized her part in what pushed him away. Not once while they talked did he get the feeling she was just telling him what he wanted to hear to get back on his good side.

He was still pondering all of this when Lavinia called out that the food was ready. When he met her in the kitchen, she had smoked turkey sandwiches with cucumber, spinach, and tomato with some barbecue chips waiting for him.

"I hope this is okay," she hedged, eying him as he approached the table. "I haven't been grocery shopping."

"This is fine." Ricky took a seat at the table.

"There's some apple pie in the refrigerator, too, if you want any."

"You made that?"

"Ha! Please. Serenity did."

"Oh."

They ate in relative silence, only making the occasional random comment. Finally, Lavinia couldn't take it anymore and put the last of her sandwich down.

"Ricky, since we're saying what's on our minds, I've gotta ask this; what does all of this mean? You being here and us having this intense conversation; what does that mean for us?"

He figured that question was coming but he still didn't have an immediate answer. His mind was still all over the place.

"I honestly don't know," he admitted, wiping his hands on a paper towel. "It's a little soon to say."

"Is there anything you *want* it to mean? Would you be open to maybe pressing pause on the divorce stuff? Or was this whole evening for nothing?"

"No, it wasn't for nothing, Lavinia. But I hope you can understand that I can't make you any promises right now. Yeah, tonight was insightful and cleansing and even changed things a *little* bit. But I'm not ready to say it shifted things enough to where we can go back to how we were."

"I don't wanna go back to how we were; we haven't been happy in years. I want us to be *better* than that. And if both of us are willing to try, I don't see why we can't be."

They sat looking at each other across the glass table.

"So leave the past in the past and start fresh; that's what you're saying?" Ricky verified after a few moments.

Lavinia nodded. "Exactly."

His tongue ran across his bottom lip. "That's something to think about. And I sincerely will. How 'bout you let me get back to you on that, all right?"

She sighed. As patient as she was telling herself to be, she didn't like hearing that she was going to be in limbo while Ricky made up his mind.

"Ricky," she hedged, "I know you. You 're gonna go back to wherever it is you're staying, report back to your therapist and probably your boys, and spend a bunch of time weighing the pros and cons of everything we talked about tonight. And all the while, I'm just sitting here waiting on pins and needles."

He quirked a brow. "Is there something wrong with weighing the pros and cons of things?"

"Sometimes you've just gotta jump in!" Lavinia exclaimed, throwing up her hands. Even though Ricky hadn't flat-out rejected her, she still somehow felt he was slipping away from her. "Everything isn't so cut-and-cry, black-and-white. This isn't a business deal; it's our marriage. And I understand you still having some reservations, but...this is one of those times when you've gotta just step out on faith, not facts and figures. Neither of us can predict the future and I'm not sitting here trying to say I'm gonna be the perfect wife from here on out, but what I *can* promise is that I won't be the same wife to you that I was before. Not after seeing and feeling what it's like to lose you."

He could see the tears glistening in her eyes, and despite himself, Ricky found himself touched by her words. What she was saying wasn't unreasonable, he realized. And she wasn't wrong about how he'd intended to handle this, as far as conferring with his therapist and friends and spending time analyzing every bit of their conversation. It was just how he operated, but that didn't mean it was the only way. Especially since he'd never seen Lavinia so humble and transparent with him, probably since they were just dating. He couldn't dismiss that, despite how much the tiny still-stubborn part of him wanted him to.

"If you're trying to get me to beg, I'm not gonna do it," Lavinia continued when Ricky didn't speak for a few moments. She crossed her arms under her breasts. "I love you more than anything, Ricky, but I'll be damned if I'm gonna grovel."

"I don't want you to grovel. I told you I'm not trying to humiliate you. This isn't some power trip for me, Lavinia. I'm just not trying to be a punk by jumping back into this with you after everything that's happened."

She frowned. "Is that what you think? Ricky, I'm not trying to make a fool out of you, I swear. That's the last thing I wanna do. Really, I hate that I've *ever* made you feel like that."

He grunted, running a hand down his face. "I just don't wanna make the wrong decision."

"You won't know if it's right or wrong until you make it." She dropped her arms. "Look...we take it one day at a time. You don't even have to move back in here right away, if you don't want to. We can talk on the phone, go on dates; court each other again. Get our communication back on track. And then just go from there."

She felt encouraged when he actually looked intrigued.

"That sounds reasonable," he admitted, gracing her with a small smile. It wasn't much and showed no teeth, but it was more than she'd gotten in forever so she'd take it. "We can try that."

Grinning, she pushed her chair back from the table and stood. Boldly taking his hand, she pulled him up with her.

"I know it'll probably be a while before the physical side of things becomes a factor – though I would love to be wrong – but can I at least have a hug?"

Ricky didn't even hesitate to oblige her. He just pulled her closer and wrapped his arms around her, immediately enjoying how her voluptuous body felt against his. It made him remember how long it had been since they slept together, and even though he didn't think going there was a good idea just yet, he was at least relieved that he was still attracted to her. During the last months before he'd left, his body hadn't been reacting to her at all, even when she walked around nearly naked.

Neither of them were in a hurry to part, but when they eventually did, Lavinia reached up and placed a hesitant hand to one cheek while she pressed her lips to the other one. Ricky closed his eyes, surprising them both by not pulling away, and they just stood there leaning into each other with their cheeks pressed together for several long moments before he finally eased back. Lavinia didn't try to push for more. She just smiled up at him and stepped back, sliding her hands down to his and giving them a squeeze before reluctantly letting them go.

"I'll call you," he told her, stepping back.

"Okay." She slid her hands into her back pockets, aching to feel his lips on hers but figuring she'd leave well enough alone. She took her own step back. "I look forward to it."

Leaving it at that, Ricky turned and headed back to the living room, grabbing his coat before heading for the door. He almost felt as if he was in a daze when he climbed into his truck and pulled out of the driveway. He was down the street and out of sight of the house before pulling over and making a call.

"You just now leaving? You sure were over there a while."

Ricky shook his head. "I'll admit it went better than I expected it to."

"I was trying to keep my hopes up but I admit I'm a little surprised to hear you say that. You and I both know how stubborn my daughter than be."

"Yeah, well...I challenged her to come correct and be honest and that's what she did. So it looks like your advice worked."

"I told you," Darla gloated. "As dramatic and extreme as it sounds, you had to actually move out and threaten to leave her for good, divorce and all, for her to get the message. I had to do the same thing with her damn daddy. Just thank the good Lord you didn't wait as long as I did to do it."

"I admit I thought you were crazy at first but it seems like you were right. I was sincerely unhappy but the bigger part of me didn't want to leave her for good. I'd just reached the end of my rope, that's all. Nothing I was saying or doing worked."

"Oh, believe me, I know."

"Thanks, Ms. Darla. Let me ask you something, though; why did you offer to help me like that? I mean, you and I aren't exactly buddies and Lavinia *is* your daughter..."

"Yeah, she's my daughter and I love her, but I also know how she is. And that stuff you heard her say that day, I knew a lot of it was probably horse dunk, if not all of it. And if you left her, I didn't want her showing up at my door with her damn bags, talking 'bout she's got nowhere else to go, even though I know she can afford her own place. 'Cause I doubt I've totally broken her daddy out of spoiling her rotten and he'd probably let her move right back in here."

Ricky burst out laughing. He might not have always wanted her in his house, but Darla was a hoot.

"And besides all that, you're a good man, Ricky," Darla continued, amusement in her voice. "You've been good to Lavinia. And I know my child would be miserable if she drove you out the door. Just like I know she's not gonna heed straightforward advice, most of the time. So sometimes, you just have to get creative."

"Well, I owe you one."

"This new big ol' TV you got us is quite enough. I'm satisfied as long as I know you're not meeting my daughter in divorce court."

"We'll see. Thanks, Ms. Darla."

Ending the call, Ricky turned up the music in his truck, glanced over his shoulder, and continued on down the street.

Chapter 20

Serenity & Taj

"Serenity?"

Shrieking, Serenity jumped and turned to face Taj, who was standing near the hallway looking at her with a slight frown. He didn't look upset, just curious.

"Taj," she breathed, pressing a hand to her chest. "I'm so sorry; I didn't see your car and didn't think you were here..."

"Oh. Yeah, my car is in the shop. I had to get a rideshare home."

"Oh...I didn't know that. I only came by because we ended up having to close the café early, and Lavinia didn't answer my text so I figured she was still with Ricky, and there weren't any movies I wanted to see in the theater. So I came by here and when I didn't see your car I figured I could just kill some time until you got back. But since you're home I can find somewhere else to go."

Taj rubbed the back of his head as Serenity grabbed her purse and started for the door. She seemed legitimately nervous around him.

"Serenity."

Slowing, she turned towards him, clearly surprised. "Yes?"

"You can hang out, if you want. I told you that you could stay here as long as you needed to."

"That's nice of you to say but I know you don't really want me here in your space, Taj. That's why I went to stay with Lavinia."

He pursed his lips and gave a slight shrug. "I'm telling you that you can hang here if you need to. It's up to you."

She eyed him as he continued on to the kitchen with the empty bowl in his hand. Truth be told, she was tired and didn't feel like finding somewhere else to go, and she couldn't afford to just cruise aimlessly around town. Staying would be the smart thing; hopefully Lavinia would respond to her text soon enough.

And Taj would likely just go back to his room, she figured. He clearly didn't really want her there; he was just trying to be a nice guy.

"All right, thanks," she muttered, going over to the couch. She heard him wash his bowl out in the sink in the kitchen and do some other moving around, but she kept her eyes on the channels she was scrolling through on the television screen.

When she heard his footsteps disappear down the hall, she released a small breath. She hated that she was so nervous around him now, and remembering why that was only made her even angrier at herself. This could be them spending a quiet evening at home if she hadn't been such a weak-minded slut.

Stop it, she silently admonished. Continuing to beat herself up wasn't doing any good. She'd apologized to everyone involved, Taj had broken up with her; she was serving her penance. She had to find a way to forgive herself, regardless of who else did.

Part of her couldn't help but wonder what Taj was doing in the room...what used to be *their* room. Shaking off that thought, she figured he was probably reading an online newspaper or some Walter Mosley novel. He loved Walter Mosley. She could just picture him on the bed – still neatly-made, of course – with his back against the headboard and his feet crossed at the ankles, absentmindedly twirling his short locs between his fingers. Sometimes he'd light some incense, but she didn't smell any.

Before she could get used to the image of herself laid next to him on the bed with her head in his lap, she shook her head and frowned harder at the television in front of her, pressing the button on the remote more aggressively than necessary.

At some point she just gave up and settled on some wrestling match. She didn't even like wrestling, but the ridiculousness of it was enough to keep her mind from wandering.

She knew one thing, though; she certainly wouldn't make the mistake of following Taj to his room like she had done to Ace that night.

She had just checked her phone for the tenth time to see if Lavinia had texted her back when Taj emerged from his room again. Her eyes stayed on her phone since she figured he was just getting something else out of the kitchen or whatever, but she felt his presence near her. Her nerves immediately returned but she forced herself not to show it; it didn't make any sense for her to be acting scared of Taj. Hopefully them being exes didn't mean they had to be enemies.

But she knew he didn't like wrestling any more than she did, so she didn't think he was standing there because he was enthralled by the television.

When he joined her on the couch, she resisted the urge to look over at him. But she allowed herself to enjoy the scent of his body oil that was wafting over to her.

"You remember the time we went to the farmers market and that woman kept following you around?" Taj suddenly asked, breaking the tense silence. "She kept insisting you were some actress that just didn't want any attention."

"Oh yeah," Serenity recalled, automatically grinning at the memory. Her phone lowered to her side. "We both kept trying to tell her that she had me mistaken for someone else but she wasn't trying to hear it."

"I almost had to call the police," Taj chuckled. "The woman just wouldn't leave you alone."

"Wow, I'd forgotten all about that...then afterwards, we got a flat tire on the way home and she rode by us, filming and laughing. I still don't know who she thought I was."

They shared a laugh that slowly tapered back into silence. Serenity still didn't know what she was supposed to say or what was even happening, so she stayed quiet.

"It helps to remember those times," Taj finally commented, tapping the fingertips of his clawed hands together in his lap. "I felt myself sliding into an ugly territory where I hated you, and I didn't want to allow myself to go there. I don't want to hate you or anyone else."

Figuring she was supposed to respond, she softly replied, "I hate the thought of you hating me. But I'd understand if you did."

"I don't hate you, Serenity." He finally looked over at her, waiting for her to return his gaze. "I...don't think I can ever get past what you did enough for us to resume our romantic relationship, but maybe at some point we can get past all this tension."

Hearing him confirm that the romantic part of their union was permanently dead sent an ache straight to Serenity's heart. She hadn't realized there had been some tiny part of her holding out hope until he said there was none. Tears pricked her eyes, but she blinked them away.

"Yeah, hopefully," she whispered.

They gazed at each other for several moments before she finally broke, turning her head to the opposite wall. Part of her wished he'd just go back to his room and leave her to watch the fake wrestling stuff in peace.

Taj had seen the tears in Serenity's eyes and it still did something to him. He didn't know if he could ever totally shut her out of his heart or his life. He hadn't said one word to Ace since learning about everything and had no plans to but he hadn't been able to keep that same energy with Serenity, at least not for very long.

He'd gone back and forth about whether or not he thought they could reconcile. Ricky was inching back into things with Lavinia, or at least trying to. From what Rasheed had told him, Ace hadn't been the only guilty one in his relationship with Charmaine, but they were working on things and were apparently still engaged. And Rasheed and Iman had finally stopped running from their obvious feelings for each other and made it official. More power to them if that's what they wanted, but every time Taj even considered giving Serenity another chance, his mind played back everything that happened. Namely the fact that he didn't learn about any of it from Serenity herself.

He wished he could hate her. He wished he could shut her out like he had Ace. When he saw her standing in his living room earlier, there was some small part of him that was happy to see her, which was why he kept finding reasons to come out of his room. Even now sitting mere feet from her, he was curious if she was still as soft as he remembered. Parts of him still craved her like he always had.

Maybe one day, down the line...

He kept those thoughts to himself, though, not wanting to get her hopes up and knowing he was still unsure as to what he wanted or didn't want, himself.

For now, sharing space on a couch would have to be enough.

THE END

Thank you so much for reading *Couple's Night*...writing this one was a roller coaster, for a few reasons. Some of these scenes were difficult but I loved the way it turned out.

However you felt about this story, please consider rating and reviewing. And if you want to show *extra* love, share that you read it on social media! ☺

You can find me on Instagram, Threads, and TikTok at @authorjessicaterry. And don't forget to subscribe to my email list at jessicaterry.com.

<u>Also by Jessica Terry</u>

Mr. Time Waster
The Stubborn Kind
From Meltdown to Mistletoe
Mrs. Soul Crusher
I Want Us
Trade Rumors
Sugar Daddy Sweet Tooth
More Than What It Is
Hooked on Valentine's
Forced
Holliday Drama
<u>The Introvert Series</u>
An Introvert's Christmas
Wooing the Introvert
The Introvert Roast
I, Take Thee Introvert
The Introvert Series Compilation (paperback only)

<u>Discussion Questions</u>

1. Each of the four couples had clear issues even before couple's night. Was there any couple that you thought might've been doomed from the beginning? Any that you rooted for?

2. What do you think of the term 'happy wife, happy life'? Does it disregard the husband, as Ricky claimed?

3. Serenity's secret weighed on her so much that it affected her physically. Did you feel *any* sympathy for her, despite her transgressions?

4. Could you understand Iman and Rasheed's reluctance to be up front about their feelings, or do you feel they dragged it out too long?

5. The four couples represented four different relationship stages; budding, long-term dating, engaged, and married. Couple's night was a turning point for each relationship. Whose issues did you feel were the most dire?

6. Forgiveness was requested among both some romantic relationships as well as the friendships. Is there any of these instances where you could see yourself granting forgiveness if the things in the story had happened to you?

7. What did you think of Ricky's method to get through to Lavinia? Was it dishonest or was it necessary?

8. Could you understand Charmaine having empathy for Serenity, after what she did? Or should she have

shut her out like Taj did Ace?

9. Was Rasheed wrong for keeping quiet about what he knew about Ace and Serenity for so long?

10. Can you see Taj taking Serenity back at some point, despite his doubts? Do you think it was unfair that Ace was given another chance in his relationship but she wasn't?

Did you love *Couple's Night*? Then you should read *Holliday Drama*[1] by Jessica Terry!

[2]

Triplets Emberly, Evelyn, Enya, and their brother Noah might be up to their eyeballs in holiday traditions and the importance of family, but their respective love lives aren't always so cheerful.

Emberly, the yearning pastry chef, considers her status as 'outcast' among her siblings as justification for the secret she's keeping.

---

1. https://books2read.com/u/38wepw

2. https://books2read.com/u/38wepw

Evelyn can't seem to accept the fact that she's divorced from her high school sweetheart, Travis, and continues to do things that are, well, foolish.

Enya has never had a problem getting a man; she's just never been pressed about keeping one. But when she finds the one she's sure is for her, he doesn't exactly come issue-free.

Serial monogamist Noah has been secretly pining for someone, and he's tired of waiting. One of his sisters might have a major problem with it, though.

All of this will come to a head at some point and when it does, will their 'family over everything' mentality withstand the damage?

Read more at https://www.jessicaterry.com/.

About the Author

Jessica Terry caught the writing bug at a young age and loves little more than holing up at home in Douglasville, GA, cranking out contemporary novels. And eating. www.jessicaterry.com

Read more at https://www.jessicaterry.com/.